THE CURSE
OF AN
ANGEL

THE CURSE
OF AN
ANGEL

NICOLE BROLLIER

authorHOUSE®

AuthorHouse™
1663 Liberty Drive
Bloomington, IN 47403
www.authorhouse.com
Phone: 1-800-839-8640

Published by AuthorHouse   07/09/2012

ISBN: 978-1-4772-4164-6 (sc)
ISBN: 978-1-4772-4163-9 (hc)
ISBN: 978-1-4772-4448-7 (e)

Library of Congress Control Number: 2012912272

PROLOGUE

Bright green-and-brown trees surrounded the soft meadow. A checkered white-and-red picnic blanket was spread across the center. Valencia and Audrey sat, enjoying a lovely lunch. A Frisbee sat on the edge of the fabric, waiting to fly.

They talked like friends, even though they were so much more. Valencia was only sixteen, and Audrey was more than double her age. They weren't mother and daughter, even though they could pass for it easily. Valencia was related to Audrey through her father. She hadn't seen him in years.

The wind picked up, swinging their hair to cover their faces. Valencia went cold when she parted hers to see the shadows. They weren't from the trees. These shadows surrounded them menacingly. Audrey moved to her niece, but a shadow grabbed her, and she disappeared from Valencia's view.

A man stepped forward. He had midnight wings to match his hair, which was pulled back into a tight ponytail. His face was pale to the point of showing the veins underneath. His eyes were a bright, fiery red. The man was wearing a suit that was perfectly trimmed and measured. In his hands was a burned scroll. With a smirk, he opened it.

"Valencia, we hereby place you under arrest. Anything you say or do will be used against you. The charges are treason. A cell has been set up for you. If you run, we have permission to hurt you. Please stand and turn around."

She obeyed, only to be placed in handcuffs. They held her roughly and took to the sky. She kept her eyes shut, hoping they wouldn't drop her. They held her exactly where she had bruises from the other night.

There was a reason she never trusted men so easily—they all turned on her, even when she needed them most. Audrey had been the one to keep her safe. She had been there when she came home tattered. Audrey was gone, and Valencia wouldn't last long.

CHAPTER 1

Wind rushed through my feathers and held my hair back. I was falling fast and had no intention of stopping soon. My wings were changing colors, and tears escaped my eyes. The pure white that was once attached to my back was ripping and tearing apart as the darkness seeped in; Heaven was farther from Earth than I remembered. I could feel the heat and intensity as I grew closer to the troposphere. Woods came into sight, and I spread my wings their whole seventeen feet. The pain and thrill slowed my descent until I landed and was able to run to a stop under the trees.

I stopped after a few stumbles and quickly drew my wings. They tucked tightly to my back as I managed to dash in a zigzag pattern for a mile. My legs were giving out from the overuse. Ducking behind a tree, I crouched very low to the ground. The very heart that caused me so much pain was beating out of my chest, slamming hard into my ribs.

I am Valencia, the daughter of an angel and demon. Like my mother, Lucia, I am an angel. I had her wing color—pure white with a violet glow, but, since my wrongful verdict, I have obtained my father's dark wings. I even have curly brown hair, thanks to him, but mine is much longer. His brown eyes are dark and fierce, yet mine have a welcoming warmth.

Unfortunately, my parents didn't last too long after my birth. They had six children before me, all of them with dark wings and the occasional horns. My birth had changed them drastically. They were used to living as outcasts—all of them. The fact that their newest child had white wings meant their fun was over. I was a complete angel, with occasional demonic bursts. At first they loved me, hoping the white was just a temporary color. A year passed, and nothing

1

changed, which made them fear the worst. Running with Mother in the fields ended, and Father had stopped all contact with me.

They wanted to bring this to the limelight in the hope that a higher-ranking demon could change my wings. Mother had run off by the time they found the appropriate demon. She had always threatened to leave my father, Evan, and in the best of their fights her main threat was leaving him for a human. It wasn't a secret; everyone knew how much she craved a human. She had returned once to see my trial. Father nearly killed the boy she had brought with her, but he knew better. I had suffered enough because of him, and the last thing I needed was to watch him destroy another life.

He had destroyed mine after Mother left. I was sent to live with his younger sister, Audrey. She and I looked very similar, so I could pass for her daughter. She had taken a better path than him. Her wings were dyed white, but her heart was pure. She'd earned her halo with pride. My life with her was magical, and she never betrayed me for a moment.

CHAPTER 2

O nce my heart slowed down and I had checked behind me a million times, I stood up straight and began to walk. The dress I was in was a deep maroon, all the way down to my ankles. It had a rounded neck, and the sleeves extended past my elbows. My skin was pale underneath. I had bare feet and no money.

Following my instincts, I went west, heading toward a camping site. When I arrived, I found an old woman with graying black hair, green eyes, and freckles. Carefully I approached with a friendly smile. I didn't startle her as I asked where I was. My eyes bore into hers, and in a slow, calm voice, I asked for a change of clothes. She welcomed me into her RV and opened a few doors before returning with sweatpants and a large jacket.

My mind control had worked yet again. I entered the cramped bathroom and was cautious when taking the dress off. When I had on the gray pants and black jacket, I left the small room. The folded-up dress in my hands was evidence of my presence. Out of thankfulness, I handed it to the woman, telling her it was one of a kind. She accepted it with a grin that warmed my heart.

After I left, my escape was on. I tried hard not to leave many footprints or stay too long in one area, which would leave scent. I did stop when the sun had dropped low enough to allow the moon to come out. I couldn't run any farther without passing out in the process. Flying to the top of a tree, I sunk into a thick branch, staying close to the main part of the tree. If luck was still on my side, the shadows wouldn't find me. They had followed me when I took off. It was their duty to capture me dead or alive.

The sun rose before I did. Panic shot through me before pangs of hunger. I dropped to the earth and began my run. I arrived at a new campsite that had breakfast going on the fire. A couple sat behind it, holding hands. The moment they saw me, they looked troubled. The woman stood and held my shoulders, pulling me to the fire. She repeated constantly that I needed to warm up and eat. She was concerned about a stranger.

I tried my hardest to be nice. The two gave me a plate of eggs and toast. My hunger took over my manners, and I wolfed the food down. After I finished I offered to stay and clean. The woman looked me over carefully and reached to pat my back. Her hand ran over the top of my left wing. Her mouth opened slightly, and then she breathed in relief; I hadn't breathed at all.

"Honey, this girl is our guardian angel."

I half-smiled and let my wings come out—before I had slept, I had used a branch to cut slits in my jacket. They didn't stretch all the way. I watched as the man sat forward in disbelief. The woman turned to me with wide eyes. "My husband has a bad back and cancer; can you cure him?"

I sat there, blinking before I nodded. Another talent of mine was healing. I walked up to the man and had him stand. He groaned but stood just enough. My fingers drifted along his spine, finding the damaged disks. I pushed just slightly to get closer. After a few minutes, he was standing taller. All that was left was to find his cancer, which was in his lungs. Standing in front of him, I shut my eyes and felt around his ribs. He'd had surgery before to see if it would help; it hadn't.

"Thank you for breakfast, but I must go." The woman came up and hugged me.

"I will take him to the doctor tomorrow to get him checked out. If you come with us I can give you a reward." The man sat again but didn't speak. He had no clue if he was dreaming or not.

"I'm sorry, I cannot stay. I hope he truly is better." I started to go to the woods once more but unfurled my wings and took to the sky.

They watched me go. Once they couldn't see me, I dropped down to the ground again. I stayed low and close to trees as I ran. Audrey would be proud that I'd helped the man. Tears welled in my eyes just thinking of her. She was a mother to me, and she had taught me everything I knew.

CHAPTER 3

My second night in the tree was more comfortable. This time I awoke to a bow with a bag of arrows. They had belonged to Audrey. The great white wood with the gold string was only a little smaller than me, and the white silk bag held each perfectly carved arrow, with a note. "My dearest Valencia, I give this to you so you can survive. Make a home here and don't forget to eat. When it is safe I will return and bring you home. Until then I have placed you in a special state making you forever young. Love, Audrey."

My heart was tight as I read. She wasn't leaving me defenseless. I placed my new weapons on my back. I floated down to the ground and began to run again. A mile went by, and I spotted deer. Crouching down, I took my shot; I hit the buck. My lessons had paid off. I got up close to remove the arrow. The buck was dead and his family had run off.

I built a fire, and I found a dropped pocketknife. I cut chunks small enough to fit on sticks and cook. What I didn't eat, I wrapped up in thick leaves and placed in the arrow case to keep safe. My stomach no longer hurt as I put the fire out.

The run was on again before the sun fell. I ate a pack of meat before resting on a new branch. My head filled with sweet dreams for the first time. I didn't worry that the shadows would come get me—there would be no way they could find me this far away. If I wanted, I could just stay here and make a life.

Chapter 4

The sun poked above the trees as I began to wake. I dropped to earth without a second glance. Instead of a run, I began to walk. I hoped I'd stumble upon something more public to find a better place to sleep. Even as I walked, I wasn't fully awake. The trees weren't coming at me as quickly as they did yesterday, which was relaxing.

Half a mile of woods passed, and I came across a highway. With discontent, I made a mad dash to the other side. Cars swerved and screeched around me, but I made it to the woods again. If I wanted I could follow along the road. Something in me screamed to go forward and obediently I followed. One thing I had learned as a child was to do as I was told. Lately, I hadn't listened, but it was time to start again.

I was deep in the woods once more when a black shadow began running past me. My brain slowed and I drew out the bow. I had an arrow at the ready when it stopped in front of me. It wasn't a horrible dark blob—it was a boy. His black wings and hair fell straight down along his back. I didn't lower the weapon when I caught his dark eyes. He was dressed in all black, from his T-shirt right down to his jeans and sneakers.

"Hello, Valencia, I am Virnant. Like your father, I am a demon, but I am here to help you. There is a cabin where I am staying. It has an extra room, if you'd join me." His voice was velvety and alluring. I lowered the bow and went to put the arrow back.

"How do you know me?"

He chuckled, coming closer. Oddly enough, I didn't feel he was trying to kill me. "I was at your trial, and I know you're innocent to your very core. They shouldn't have taken your halo. It'd be a great honor to assist you."

He half-bowed, and I nodded to him. "One night; I can't impose."

His head shook as he led me deeper into the woods. I watched my surroundings until the cabin came into view. It was small but made of complete wood logs. For a moment, it was like being back in Heaven, listening to Abraham Lincoln talk about his house.

The cabin's inside was larger than I'd expected. The first room was a den filled with couches, chairs, a coffee table, and a TV. Virnant took me deeper into the home. The kitchen was large and spotless, with whites and blacks and the occasional silver. He turned on his heels and took me to my room. I was stunned as I looked at a large bed with an ocean of pillows. It had a great view, with French doors leading to a porch.

"This is all too much. How could I repay you?" He came up next, to me looking me in the eyes. His seemed to go on forever.

"All I want is for you to be safe and allow me to train you."

I walked into the room and up to the bed. My only belongings fell upon the bed as I turned to him. "Train me how?"

His smile grew a tad bigger as he came close. "You are on the run, in danger. The least I could do is show you how to fight. If it will make you feel better, you can repay me by obeying me."

As I looked at him, my eyes grew in wonder. I had my suspicions, but he seemed kind. "I thank you, Virnant. Here, I have some meat from a deer left. You might like it, it's rather fresh." My hands searched the pack before I pulled out the leaf packages. His chuckle filled the room as he took his gift. The whole time he was careful not to let our fingers touch. Word had definitely traveled far.

"Go to that closet; I took the liberty of having clothes in your size delivered. I do hope you like them." The door opened under my fingers, and my jaw dropped. Dresses were in the far right, followed by sweaters and jackets. To the left were T-shirts and jeans. Out of pure routine, I reached for a dress. The silk met my fingers first. I pulled a pink dress from the hanger and held it to my body.

"There has to be a way to thank you. You barely know me—why do any of this?"

He came close but chose to sit on the bed instead. "Your story has been told by many, and I hope you can share with me the truth. It is a true tragedy when looked at in a certain light. Of all the things you have gone through, you haven't experienced Earth. Not enough are nice, but you need kindness—and I am here to show you what that is." Inside I knew what he wanted most, but I denied it to myself in hopes I was seeing it wrong.

Ignoring what I wanted to originally ask, I queried about the bathroom. He pointed to the door near the entrance to my room. I had a private bathroom.

There was a shower and a toilet and a large mirror above the sink. Quickly I put on the dress. The arms stretched past my shoulders, and the edges were hemmed with flowers that were still fresh. It went a few inches past my knees, and the neck was close to my collar. For a few minutes I twirled in the mirror, wishing I could fix my hair. Its curls had started to straighten out and tangle. Next to the sink was a hairbrush and a hair tie. I pulled my hair up, and I came out.

Virnant was still there, waiting for me. His eyes lit up, and I smiled. He stood up and walked around me. My cheeks flared red. After a few circles, he stopped in front of me.

Chapter 5

Virnant's eyes bore into mine. I looked up, making my face go blank. For a few moments, I tried to see if I could press into his brain; I couldn't. The room was silent—even the outdoors hadn't made a noise.

"Tell me a story, Valencia."

I moved to the bed and sat down. He stayed put, knowing better. It was not a secret that my "daddy issues" had made me freak out at any male affection. Honestly, it didn't bother me. It was just the fact that I couldn't control it, especially when the word *no* had never worked. I wasn't afraid to the point I'd never date a boy; there were the rare times when a special angelic boy would steal a kiss. It was the demonic ones I didn't trust; they were the kind I grew up with.

"Which one?" I asked.

He came a step closer. "How about one of Evan; I had known him long ago."

My head rang, and I pulled my legs up to tuck under me. Carefully, I let my wings stretch out and rest. Each feather extended and relaxed as I tried to pick out a story. "You know he's my father, and he gave me to his sister. Before he left me, he tried to teach me to fly. Our first lesson, he tossed me out the third-floor window. Below were my eldest sister and brother. They were holding out a mattress stuffed with cotton in place of springs. I stayed aloft for a minute before I spiraled down. To this day, I remember the pain and then the laughs before mother ran out and held me. She set me down and walked off, along with the others."

I watched him smile a tad. Slowly, he turned and walked into the closet. He crouched down and searched toward the back. When he did return, his outstretched hands contained shoes. They were simple black flats.

"May I, Valencia?" My heart escalated, and I nodded. One by one, my feet appeared. I could tell Virnant was trying to prove he was different. "Thank you for the story, may I tell you one?" Another nod followed as he bent down, reaching my right foot. I bit hard on my lips, breaking skin. Blood filled my mouth, and I tried my hardest not to scream. My fingers dug deep into the bedding as the shoe slid on. Once he was finished, his hands retreated rapidly, and he looked up at me. "It is true; you do fear the touch of man."

I shook my head and pulled my foot back to me. "No, I just don't trust the demonic touch. You can put on the last one if you want while you tell the story."

His mood perked up, and he lifted the last shoe. He was extra delicate when putting it on. "Before your mother met Evan, I knew him. I also knew Audrey; she was always a fun spirit. We had been friends, and Audrey was determined to get her halo. Evan wanted to live up to meet Lucifer—that is until he met Lucia. One night, we had gone down to the town, and Audrey had run off with some boy she had her eyes set on. Your father was determined to find some girl. That night, he met your mother. His eyes lit up, and she was decked out in a blouse and a skirt. She was nothing like you. He was in love instantly, and it was the last time I saw him for a long time. Well, I was at the wedding briefly, and then your trial." The shoe slid on, and he stood up. I thanked him and started to stand. "Let me get you some food. Please go rest in the living room."

As I agreed to before, I obeyed. I sat on the couch and waited patiently. Time ticked by before he sat next to me, handing me a plate with a grilled cheese. He placed an ice tea on the table in front of us. His own plate sat on his lap as he watched me eat.

The warmth was welcoming, and the yellow cheese gooed out. It was delicious with every crunch. There was something in between the slices of cheese, but I couldn't quite describe it. Once the sandwich was gone, the drink came next. It was unsweetened, just how I liked it. A lemon wedge floated among the ice cubes that shimmered to the bottom. After he finished, I took his plate.

As I walked to the sink, Virnant followed me. He sat at a small table and watched me intently. Water rushed over my hands, and a sponge released bubbles. I smiled as I cleaned each plate and then the glasses. As the water hit my hands, I remembered helping Audrey after every dinner. She would wash, and I dried. I would sit on the counter with the cabinet open so I could put the dishes away.

CHAPTER 6

My smile only grew by the time I finished. I returned each dish and cup before looking out the window. The sun had set yet again. Virnant stood and joined my side; he stayed his distance, knowing better. I had already let him push boundaries.

"Tomorrow, I would like to start training so sleep well." I left him there with a nod. My door shut behind me, and I walked to the French doors. Making sure they were locked, I pulled the shades over them. In the closet, I found a nightgown. It was baby blue, and it went to my knees and wrists.

In the sea of pillows, I was toasty warm. It did not take me long to fall asleep. This time, I felt safe—that was until I landed into a nightmare. My screams rang only in my head. My feet beat against pavement as I ran down a dark road. The shadows were following me. Their massive forms were bigger than my five-and-half-foot-tall body. For eyes, they had darker holes with a tint of red. The largest had to be eight feet and toppled upon me in several bounds. My wings could not save me.

I awoke in a cold sweat and shot straight up. My final scream echoed off the walls. All my hair had fallen from the tie and ended up stuck to my face. As I tried to catch my breath, the door opened. Virnant stood in front of me with his wings open and a fire poker in his left hand. He was half-asleep and his hair hung down to his collarbone.

"What's wrong?"

I blushed, turning away. He didn't have a shirt on, only pajama pants. "Nightmares are back. I'm so sorry to have disturbed you. Next time, I will control myself."

The tension eased careful away as he relaxed. He set the long object next to my door. "No, it is all right, I expect you to have nightmares. Would you like to talk about it?"

With a little adjustment, I pulled a pillow up to rest upon. "I'm fine. You should sleep, you look exhausted."

He stumbled closer and sat at the edges of the bed. "I don't sleep much. Do you mind if I stay in here for a bit? Something feels off. You can sleep; I won't bother you."

Against my will I nodded. He had done so much for me, and it was the least I could do after waking and terrifying him.

With reservations, I went deeper into the covers, tucking them in close. I felt him shift and pull at one of the pillows. He left the bed, but lay down on the floor. My shoulder blades eased back, and my closed eyes flickered open briefly. Sleep was difficult to achieve, but I managed.

I awoke alone; he had gone. Briefly, I pinched my arm to see if I had only dreamt of Virnant. After a few blinks, I was still safe in the bed. Ripping the covers off, I set my feet on the cold floor. Silently, they moved along the floor to the bathroom.

A warm shower woke me up. Instead of searching for a blow dryer, I settled with braiding my hair. The towel stayed around me as I went to search for clothes for the day. While I was in the closet, the main door opened. My body steadied itself and I went to reach for my bow.

CHAPTER 7

Everything happened fast, but I spun in time to dodge his attack. Virnant was laughing beside me. Frustration got the best of me and I punched his shoulder.

"Lesson one: be prepared for everything, and I can safely say you were ready."

I smiled and then nearly shrieked. In a mad dash, I was back in the bathroom. He chuckled, and I listened as he left the room. I went back out and changed into jeans and a T-shirt.

After I left my room, he was waiting for me in the kitchen. The scent of bacon hit me first before I saw the toast spring to life. He was busy as I went into the kitchen. In an attempt to help him, I managed to set up plates and orange juice on the table. We enjoyed our little breakfast, not allowing a word to pass between us. In a way, it was nice.

His eyes even refrained from looking at me. "To train, you can't tense up at every touch. It will be harder to fight back. Also, you'll be easier to capture. We don't have to physically touch, but in battle it's a contact sport."

That's one thing I wasn't looking forward to. There was no avoiding it. It was time to break my shell or return for punishment. "Can we ease into it?"

His smile was soft when he looked at me. I returned it and finished off my toast.

Like yesterday I took our dishes and washed them. This time, he joined in and dried them. He stayed close to see if it'd help. His left wing tapped my right, and if my skin didn't crawl it would be a miracle. Virnant caught my distress and moved over.

"Valencia, I do understand you are uncertain of me. You also don't like the fact that I was your father's friend. Don't forget, I also was acquainted with Audrey."

I shut the water off and handed him the last glass. I dried my hands on a free towel and turned to lean against the counter. "I never heard of you and do not remember seeing you. Please do not take it to heart if I accidentally upset you."

He finished on the glass and put it away. The towel he held dropped onto the counter in a heap as he looked me over as if he had missed something. "You had so much potential when you were born. It has all been destroyed by his foolish mistakes. I had tried to warn him, but he only shunned my existence in your life. Evan was a tough man, and all his children were precious to him. You made him rethink his life. Your birth alone was full of great power. If he had kept you and allowed me to teach you, we wouldn't be here." He sighed and walked away, leaving me to think. His bedroom, door shut and I went out the front.

With a running start, I was airborne. I would return after I thought everything over. Virnant had planned ahead and made slits in every top he'd given me for the days I would fly off. Thoughts vibrated in my skull as the wind pushed my cheeks back. Father had always been strict when I knew him, but I never knew he had banned people from my life.

The ground below looked friendly for the first time. Ascending higher, I spotted a new cabin, with cars were parked around it. I watched as teens piled into the cabin. I hovered and looked at them. There were six in total, plus the one adult I saw.

If I wasn't upset, I would have flown closer. I moved farther east, catching a glimpse of another cabin. There were no lights on, just cars. To the left were a few tents being set up. There were more teens, who looked closer to my age, sixteen, than the others I saw.

After passing a few abandoned cabins, I decided to turn back. My thoughts had eased down, and I was much calmer. Making a U-turn, I flew over each one again. They all looked the same as before. I had made it to mine right as the sun had begun to set; I must have gone farther than expected.

CHAPTER 8

Dinner was waiting for me when I returned. The smell of chicken roamed around the rooms, and I followed my nose to the kitchen. There was a plate set up with two slices of chicken and a glob of mashed potatoes. Next to my fork and knife was a note. I shook out my exhausted wings and began to read.

"Valencia, I am sorry if I upset you. I ran out to attend a meeting with a few friends. It shouldn't take long so make yourself comfortable. Virnant."

I let the note remain next to me as I ate. It was delightful, and the potatoes were heavenly.

I cleaned my dish and silverware once I was done. Instead of waiting for his return, I went to my room. The nightgown went on once more, and I sat there, braiding my hair again, in hopes to obtain my curls once more. When the pigtails were finished, I sat in the darkness.

For a while, I felt suspended, as if I had been put on pause. No thoughts ran through my head, and I didn't move except my chest went up and down to get at the air. It was the sound of the door that had pulled me from my odd state. He had returned and was knocking. It opened slowly, and he turned on the light as he entered.

"Did you have a nice meeting?" He looked ragged and on the verge of passing out but nodded instead. His feet pulled him deeper into the room and I stayed put on the bed.

"One of my friends came down for a visit. He brought a few of his kids with him."

I half-smiled and knew better than to push for names.

Instead of silence, he continued to speak as if he hadn't for a long time. "He and I talked for a while before he brought you up in the conversation. His first question was your appetite."

My eyebrows raised in shock. "What could possibly be wrong with my eating habits?"

He looked me over, and I could tell he was thinking I was blind to the truth. His mouth opened and shut several times before he came closer. He didn't bother sitting near me and remained standing, even though it was clear his legs hurt. "When an angel's halo is taken, not only do her wings turn black, but her sanity retreats along with any power she once had. The worst that comes of it if she falls to earth is that she can smell the blood under their skin. Not only does it drive her wild, but she hungers for it until she can have it and one drop will not satisfy."

I was trembling by the end. My wings closed around me, and I saw the darkness of each feather; they were white just days ago. A hand patted my head; I couldn't feel the halo. Tears welled in my eyes. I slithered away from him turning my back to him.

A rough hand touched where my wings connected to my back. To me, I could feel every feather burning, but to him it must have felt soft and comforting. I tucked in tighter, craving to move away.

"My friends can help you." His voice was calm and soothing, but I shook my head.

"I want to sleep. Can we talk tomorrow?"

His hand tightened a little, but withdrew. He said goodnight and walked out the door. That night, I slept in a tight ball with my bow next to me.

CHAPTER 9

As I stirred, I heard Virnant cooking again. I slipped into another dress. This one was black, past my knees with sleeves just inches past my shoulders. The neck was square and not too low. To finish, I put on the black flats once more.

I left my room and he was setting our plates down. On each one was a chicken sandwich, still steaming. He had a bottle of water next to my plate this time. After I sat down, we began to eat. Virnant didn't push for further discussion about my appetite. Instead he only brought up training. I agreed that we could start today.

Once we had cleaned our plates, I was sent to change. I followed his suggestions and put on shorts and a tank top, as much as I disliked it. They would be a much better choice and wouldn't get in the way. There were sneakers in the back of the closet that were blue like my offit.

As I left the house, he sprang on me. My arms went up to push him back, but I had already hit the ground. He hovered above me before he landed. His wings were longer than mine by a at least yard. He lowered his hand to help me. I lifted mine, and he pulled me to my feet. "We'll go easy today."

I nodded, and he came at me again instructing me how to block. We flew upward a little to make it a greater challenge. With every touch, my teeth grinded harder. By lunch, I didn't mind the occasional contact when I messed up.

We stopped briefly for sandwiches and water. As we flew upward again, he taught me an easy attack—if I gained enough speed and came at a downward angle with my leg outstretched, even if my foot missed, I could lower a fist quickly to at least contact a wing or his head. Over and over we went through this until I was able to make him sink lower.

The last of the chicken vanished into our growling stomachs. We had gulped down three-and-a-half bottles of water each. My wings ached as I dragged myself to the shower. He stayed put, looking more energetic than me. The warm water was a pleasant sensation that slowly soothed me to the point that I could sleep almost anywhere.

Instead of the nightgown, I found a T-shirt and crawled in bed. The pillows had the texture of cotton, and the slight breeze from under the door was relaxing. It truly didn't take long to sleep, I was so worn out. Before I shut my brain off, I had heard Virnant retire to his room. I still hadn't seen it, but I knew it was close to mine.

Unfortunately, I had a new nightmare. Father had found me. He took me back to have my wings cut. That was the punishment for betrayal. I had been accused of selling secrets to Lucifer and secretly meeting with him. Never once had I seen him in person. He did send me a letter when I was on trial. His offer was my rescue, where I would be safe if I devoted everything to him. If I was worthy he would make me his wife. That alone scared me senseless.

CHAPTER 9

Screams awoke me, and I realized they were my own. This time Virnant didn't come running. As I sat up, I stretched my wings out as far as I could until the tips touched the walls. Shaking them out, I stood and entered the bathroom. Cold water ran over my face until my heart rate lowered enough so I could sleep again.

The next time I awoke, Virnant was standing in the doorway. He had an odd look in his eyes, but didn't move. I only sat up and said his name. His head cocked to the side, and he stumbled in.

"Are you going to allow my friends to help you?" His bluntness made me smile a tad.

"I would rather keep my whereabouts on a low profile. Thank you for everything, though." With a nod, he walked away. Instead of chasing him down, I got up to shut the door.

By the time I went out to help with breakfast, I had changed into sweatpants and a T-shirt, with a jacket tied to my waist. The weather here changed daily. As I began to help him set the table, he had cooked another batch of scrambled eggs. As if by habit, we ate without a word.

Words weren't passed until we were cleaning the dishes. He wanted to test my speed both on land and in the air. We left quickly through the front door in a sprint. He was faster than me; I could still faintly see him dodging trees before he was up in the air. When my feet hit where he took off, I sprung upward, getting at least ten feet before opening my wings. Pushing down hard was a good exercise for them.

We whirled past each other multiple times. Our position changed rapidly, and I could hear him chuckle softly often. When I did catch up to him, I heard screams. My head dropped down to see a boy pinned under a tree by his leg and arm. His group of friends surrounded him, pulling out cell phones and trying to see if they had bars.

Virnant had disappeared, allowing me to drop down. I pulled the jacket tight over my wings and hurried to the crowd. They were the second group I had seen. and none of them looked at me until I was sitting next to the boy. The left side of his body was trapped.

CHAPTER 10

The boy had blond hair to the bottom of his ears, and he was pale as a ghost. His blue eyes looked me over repeatedly. He hadn't spoken a word to me, but the group looked over in silence. I motioned to two of the other boys to push at the tree with me while the four girls held him still. It took five minutes for all of them to agree and begin to help.

We ignored his screams, but managed to get the tree off. Once his breathing and heart rate had slowed, I lifted him with ease. I asked for directions to their cabin, even though I knew the way. My wings were clenched to my back while I ran my right hand secretly over every shred and gouge in his arm and leg. The bleeding stopped, and the wounds looked like they had been there a day or two. I stopped, seeing how I couldn't do more.

The other teens didn't speak as I brought him in the house and set him on the couch. It had been the first thing I had seen. The inside was similar to the one where I was staying, except the kitchen had more dirty dishes. The boy grabbed my wrist so I couldn't walk away.

"What's your name?" His voice was small and dry.

Before I answered, I had the tallest girl go get him water. "Valencia, what is yours?"

His pupils opened proving my name wasn't common here. "My name is Mark. Do you camp around here?" The red head had brought him water. I let him drink it before I answered. He gulped it down hungrily, as if he had eaten sand earlier.

"No, it's my first time out here. I better get going before my . . ." That's where I bit my tongue. In a few moments I found a suitable word, " . . . *uncle* comes looking." The small group eyed me as I went to the door. Mark's voice speaking my name filled the room. All heads turned to him as I walked closer.

"Don't go. You can call on the main phone."

My smile faltered slightly. I had no clue if we had a phone in the cabin.

"Can someone get him fresh clothes, a cold rag and maybe some medicine?" With that response, I went and sat next to him, but on the floor.

His hand reached for mine, and I let it wrap around my fingers. As much as I disliked the touch, he needed comfort.

"Where do you go to school? I haven't seen you before." I looked away and up at the remaining three; two guys and a girl. The two boys had brown and black hair, but the girl was a blonde, like the other, making me assume they were twins.

"I don't go to school." The shock caught him off guard, but he smiled. "How old are you Mark?" His name was so simple, and it wouldn't be hard to remember at all.

"Seventeen in a week, what about you?" I watched his dimples fade as he went to move his arm. He almost shrieked, but squeezed my hand instead, making me jump up. "I'm so sorry, I didn't mean to hurt you." His hand slithered away in disappointment.

"No, it's my fault. I shouldn't have reacted badly. I'm sixteen." With that, the others returned. Each girl held something different. The black-haired girl held his clothes, and the blonde had a cold rag. It was the redhead who held a pill container.

The two boys lifted him and put him in his room, helping him change. Thankfully he had been given a T-shirt and sweats, so I could I work around the materials. The boys were in the same room I had in my cabin. The only differences were the two extra beds all of which were twins and the suit cases scattered around.

I gave him the bottle, unsure of what it was. He took two white pills with a fresh glass of water. As he was propped up on some pillows, I examined the cuts. His arm was broken.

"Where did you learn all this if you don't attend school?"

It would be impossible to explain how medical aid was important to gaining a halo. "TV, I watch enough and read just as much. Can someone get me tweezers?" I ran the rag over his wounds to hide the truth of what I was doing. To my amazement, I couldn't fix the broken bone. I had always been able to mend those.

The tallest blonde gave me tweezers, and I pulled out bark and wood from Mark's arm. His mouth was clenched tight, as if on fire. When I finished with his arm, I reported it was broken. The smallest girl with black hair was off to call the doctor.

I moved down and rolled up his left pants leg. His leg wasn't broken, just badly impaired. There was less bark here, which made me grin. Once I was done, I looked over each person in front of me. The two blonde girls had the same light-green eyes, along with the same tan. If they weren't twins with same white hair, then they had to be friends since birth. The redhead had dark green eyes that reminded me of a cat. With a soft giggle, I looked at the last three. They all had brown eyes.

"I'm going to go. It was nice to meet you all." I started to leave again, but one of the guys stopped me by stepping in front of me; he was much bigger than I was.

"Come by tomorrow. I'm sure he'd like to thank you."

His muscles must have been bigger than my head. He wore a football jacket, which explained it all.

"I don't know if I can. My uncle doesn't even know I'm here."

The girl with black hair nearly pounced on me she came so close. "He would die if he couldn't thank you. I'll make dinner, do you like lasagna?"

I smiled and agreed. Her arms wrapped around me. I patted her back before leaving. When I was a safe distance, I took off.

CHAPTER 11

Virnant was at home, waiting for me. He approved of my good deed and even said I could visit after training. We had dinner—microwave mac and cheese. It came in small plastic bowls, which meant our forks were the only thing we'd have to wash. When we had finished eating, I retreated to my room. The bed caught my eyes and sucked me in instantly. I was asleep on impact.

I awoke to no sounds from the kitchen. With a small shrug I got in the shower. I made several tight braids after I got out—they would help with my curls later tonight. This time when I left Virnant was getting up to go cook. Instead I offered and won cooking the eggs.

He sat with a smile until I came over. To my surprise he actually enjoyed them. It warmed my heart. We finished and washed our dishes. This time he washed and I dried. When I looked into the cabinets I noticed there was at least four of everything.

"Today I just want you to relax and do an endurance flight. It won't strain you, so you can attend the dinner."

My smile grew, and I gave him a hug. The contact of his skin burned and itched in my head. When I was done, I was out the door. He followed me into the sky and had me go to the top of the troposphere. The air was nice, but he didn't urge me to go higher.

Instead, he had me go faster. He had me test my limits until we descended down. It was lunchtime. He touched the ground but had me stay hovering. When he returned I hadn't moved in any direction. He had a granola bar in his hand.

I came down and took it as I went to change. His smile showed how much this meant to him in some way. After I entered my room, the door shut. I dug through the closet and found a dark blue dress. It came to my knees and almost to my elbows. The neck was rounded and somewhat low. The material was warm and felt like cotton. I took out each braid and ran my fingers through my hair. The curls fell at random and hung around my head, but bounced with each step.

Virnant knocked, and opened the door slightly until I admitted him. His smile grew when caught sight of me. "You look lovely, but is it a fancy dinner?" I shrugged slightly. Dinner with Audrey had always been a time I could dress up. "Either way, I found heels that strap on. Be careful, I don't need you snapping an ankle." He chuckled, and I sat on the bed.

As he came close, he showed me the black, one-inch heels. They had bows on top and a small strap around the ankle. He bent down and slid them on. This time my heart accelerated and that was it. There was no burn to his touch and my fingers weren't dug deep in the bedding. My shell was cracking.

He gave me a tiny hug before I took off. I circled the illuminated house. I floated until I was in view of it and landed a quarter mile away. I stopped and held a tree trunk, gripping it tightly. My wings merged into my back, so they wouldn't be spotted easily.

I knocked on the door, and Mark opened it. He welcomed me inside, and I stepped in slowly, looking around. We were alone. My heartbeat increased as I came in closer. I turned to look at him; his arm was in a sling, and he had a slight limp. His free hand pointed toward the kitchen. My gaze followed, and my breathing stopped. A table was set with candles.

"Stephanie said she'd cook for us, and the others said they'd sleep in the tents tonight. You remember Stephanie? She had black hair and hugged you." We walked into the kitchen, and he hurried ahead of me, holding out my seat. He had on a dress shirt, but dark sweats and sneakers. I sat down, and he pushed the chair into a comfortable place.

"This is unbelievable! Whose idea was it?"

His cheeks turned pink as he went to the microwave and pulled out a dish. He set it in front of me. It was a hunk of lasagna, as promised. "I wanted to thank you, and the girls suggested a dinner. You look beautiful by the way, how did you know to dress up?" He turned to get his plate as I blushed.

"I lived with my aunt, and every night we would dress up even if it was just us."

He sat across from me and grinned.

"How's your arm?" I asked as I picked up my fork and took a small bite. The warm cheese oozed with a scrumptious taste. The pasta was soft and smooth. There was a thin layer of sauce, just the way I liked it.

"Doctor was astonished I had survived, and the weirdest part was he said I looked healed—that there should be more blood." I looked down and lifted a few more forkfuls. Mark was shoveling in the food, since he had a larger slice.

"That's amazing, Mark, I'm glad to hear it. Why isn't your arm in a cast? Isn't it broken?"

I continued to eat, and he began to talk. His words lifted my hope slightly. "It is broken, but it's in the final stages of healing. He said a sling would be fine."

As I continued to eat, I smiled. I glanced over his shoulder and out the window. A face was poking up, just enough to see us. She had a rim of black hair, making me smile and give a slight wave to Stephanie.

Mark caught my gesture and glanced back, making her disappear. "I'm sorry, she just isn't used to me meeting a girl that I like." His face went bright red, and he looked down. The fork he held didn't move.

"Mark, don't be embarrassed. I know how you feel. I've never really liked guys before. This is my first date." That was true. I had a guy friend before, but when he liked me I couldn't stay. It ended our friendship, even though he was my first kiss.

"When you finish, I'd like to take you on a walk. Is there a time you have to be home?"

I finished chewing and swallowed. "He didn't give me a time, so I have until I get tired." I watched his face light up as he finished off his final bite. My fork lifted the last bit, and I savored it.

"The girls would love it if you slept over one night, like a sleepover—maybe tomorrow. We have all week here, then every weekend." As I patted my lips with the napkin he was already taking the plates and dishes. I stood up and went to help him wash. He didn't pull out a sponge or soap; he only set them on other dirty dishes.

I bit my tongue but went to answer him. "That sounds wonderful, should I bring anything special?"

He smiled and leaned against the counter to face me. I ignored my strong impulse to reach into the sink and begin to clean. "Unless the girls want to sleep outside again, you'll be inside, so I say bring anything comfortable, and it won't be too fancy." With a smile I nodded. He lifted his right hand and left it midair. His eyes danced from mine to his hand, until I took it. He gave a slight squeeze and led me to the front door.

I opened it for us and closed it once he walked out. He led me down the driveway, walking at a slow pace, as if I could fall at any moment. That's when I realized why mother liked humans so much. They got shy when they liked you, and they didn't act like they owned you. Of course, I knew there had to be some out there, but Mark was trying to be nice, ignoring the fact I had helped save him.

"Valencia, where did you come from?"

My grip on his hand loosened just enough, but I didn't release him completely. "Don't laugh—I fell from the sky."

He smiled instead and playfully bumped into me.

"I'm being serious, what state or country did you come from?"

That's when I dropped his hand, but smiled bigger. I twirled away, but walked backward in front of him. "This will sound harsh, but there are things some don't understand. Once I know you better, I can accept you into my world with open arms. Just please, don't push."

He nodded and went to speak, but shut his mouth so he could think again. I returned to his side, and we walked onto a road.

"May I walk you home?" He had gotten upset.

I could feel the tears forming, but blinked them away quickly. "I don't know which cabin is mine. If I angered you, I am sorry. It's just, there are things in my life I can't share."

In an instant he stopped in his tracks and let go of my hand. I stood in front of him so I could see him better in the darkness. "You aren't a fugitive are you?" My fists clenched, and I bit my lip. He saw he struck a nerve and reached to pull me into a hug. "Valencia, I meant it as a joke to lighten the mood. I didn't mean it to offend you."

I nodded. "I will see you tomorrow, Mark. Just consider that there are things that you can't share with people, especially strangers." I took off in a full sprint. He stayed put, and I was airborne when he couldn't see me. Kicking a shoe off, I aimed it for where he stood. If he was smart, he'd catch the hint.

CHAPTER 12

On my way home, with tears streaming my face, I caught a glimpse of black wings. It came from the cabin I had first seen. I paused in midair and blinked. Assuming it was a crow, I hurried my flight. Virnant was outside, waiting for me, when I landed. He gave me a hug before he sent me to bed. Words didn't pass between us, but he knew what was wrong.

After I was settled in, he entered with milk and cookies. All of which were piping hot. My mood perked up a bit as he sat next to me. He rested the plate on my lap, but held the milk.

"Did you want to talk about it?" I lifted up a cookie. It was chocolate chip. Carefully I bit in. The chocolate melted on impact, and the dough was chewy.

"He asked if I was a fugitive." I finished off the cookie and looked at Virnant.

"What did you tell him?" His eyes were wide.

I ate another cookie, but he wouldn't touch them. "I didn't tell him the truth—just said he had to consider there are things he doesn't know." That's when he lifted a cookie and ate it. There were two left, so I had one more, and then spoke. "The girls wanted me to sleep over there tomorrow. I said I'd go, are you okay with that?"

He nodded and took the plate. After handing me the milk he left.

It was still hot when I drank it. The glass emptied quickly. Impulse had me stand up and walk to the kitchen. The glass was clean, and I could sleep. As I headed back to bed I heard Virnant's voice. He was in his room. Curiosity got the best of me, and I walked closer so I could hear. For a minute, it was silent, and then he was talking about meeting with someone tomorrow. He slammed the phone down.

I went straight to my room. Once under the covers, I slept. Periodically, I awoke and saw Virnant in the doorway. I couldn't stay awake long enough to talk once I spotted him. When morning came, I fully awoke. I went to the kitchen and cooked.

He came out once I was done. We ate in silence, and I didn't dare mention his phone call. As we cleaned our plates, he claimed to have something for me. My smile formed with ease, and he left me where I was to go get it.

He came back with hands behind his back. I had stopped putting the dishes away by then. "Valencia, I know this is definitely not you, but this is what most human girls wear, and you don't have it in your closet." His hand came around holding a blue bag. With a chuckle, he opened it reached in. Out came jean shorts, and I was gasping for air. Out of respect, I grabbed the material and thanked him. "The bag is yours too; you can put in anything you need for the night." Thanking him again, I took everything and went to my room. He hadn't mentioned training at all.

I went to change. The shorts were at least half a foot long. I dug through the closet for a top. I choose a sweater, so at least some of me was covered. It had black-and-gray stripes running horizontally. After brushing out my hair and putting on sneakers, I packed my bag. Shorts weren't included in tomorrow's outfit.

Virnant was waiting for me in the living room. He smiled and stood up. I stayed put as he began to speak, "Let me drive you. I can pull the concerned uncle act. Besides, I want to know which cabin you're at, in case I need you." With a nod, he led me out side. A Lamborghini sat in the driveway; the black paint shined under the sun.

Once we were inside, he sped away burning rubber. It was like flying, but in a small area. As we passed one cabin, I saw dark curls bounce down its driveway. Shrugging it off, he pulled up to the right place. He took my bag and walked up to the door. His fist hit it softly, and it opened quickly. Stephanie came outside and pulled me into a hug.

"Mark's outside and the others are eating. Hello, you must be her uncle. I'm Stephanie." She reached out to shake his hand, and I smiled. He walked in after taking it. As she shut the door she caught a glimpse of the car, and her eyes bugged.

"I am Virnant. It is nice to meet you. Valencia, you can go find Mark if you want." With a nod, I left him standing there. He was telling her when he'd be by to pick me up tomorrow. I went out the back door, and Mark was sitting on the steps, looking into the woods. Instinct had me sit next to him.

"I'm sorry if I hurt you, Valencia." I shrugged it off, telling him not to worry. He got up and walked to the blue tent. I stayed put when he came back, holding my high heel. "This hit my head last night. It looked like yours." My cheeks flamed as I took the shoe.

"Thank you. It came off when I was headed home. What are we doing tonight?" He smiled and sat next to me again.

"Well, Cinderella, the girls wanted to sleep in the tents again, so it'll be like a regular camping trip."

I smiled brightly. I knew all the fairytales. Cinderella escaped and got the prince. If only that was true for me. "Tell me something about you, Mark—do you have any siblings?"

He stood up soundlessly and took my hand. We walked into the woods as he began to speak. "I have a younger sister; her name is Wendy. My parents split last year, so I don't see her often. She stays with my mom."

My heartbeat was a little slower, knowing his pain. "My parents aren't together either. Actually after my mother left, I was sent to live with my aunt. My father couldn't handle all seven of us."

Mark gasped at the number, and I smiled a tad more. In my head, I assumed large families weren't common here. "You have six siblings?" His jaw was hanging a little, and I couldn't tell if he was jealous or stunned. I just nodded with a small, agreeable noise.

"I'm the baby of the group, and I haven't lived with them since I was about one." This time, he laughed softly, as if he couldn't believe me. "I know it's weird, but their names are just as weird as mine." He shook his head.

I let him lead us deeper in the woods. He talked of his family more and didn't push when I wouldn't tell a lot. His mother had cheated, because his father was never home, and he still wasn't. When he was, he was drunk. Mark was lucky though—his dad didn't want him dead, just his mother.

We made it to a little creek and sat down. I sat on his left side and took the arm from the sling. His eyes watched me carefully as

I ran my fingers over the skin. I could feel the bone and the crack. I tried hard for five minutes, but nothing happened. Feeling defeated, I looked into Mark's eyes. I tried to get him to stand, but he only adjusted himself. My powers were gone. My wings tucked in tighter as I stood.

CHAPTER 13

If I wasn't already headed back with him, I would have flown off. I didn't need to frighten him, though. We arrived to a group outside, gathering wood and twigs. Mark began to introduce everyone, so I would know who was who. The tallest boy was Tom, and the smaller one was Spencer. The twins were Tiffany and Tina, the smallest. The redhead was Mary. I already knew Stephanie, and she knew me, even though Mark repeated my name again so they would all know.

We joined the small circle, just as I noticed the sun was low. Our walk must have been longer than expected. Instead of worrying about time, I offered to help. They were already taking care of everything, so my help wasn't needed. Instead, we all sat, and occasionally one of them would ask me a question. Again, I gave the same answer to where I was from and was greeted by laughs.

The sun stooped lower, and the fire was lit. Sticks were passed out, along with a bag of marshmallows. I helped Mark with his before I took one of each for myself. Something about this act bewildered everyone. My cheeks steamed as I put the stick in the fire. Spencer was the first to ask for a scary story. My head dug deep trying to think of something, but Tom stood, flashlight in hand.

For a half-hour, he babbled about a hooked man. If his voice had gone along with every word, and he put in a correct pause, I'd have reacted better, but he only prattled on. It was Tina who played along to make him happy. When the story ended, Mark put an arm around my shoulders. I pulled my wings in tight and bit my tongue as I leaned in closer.

Stephanie stood, and her bright eyes darkened. Her voice went low and eerie. "Steven Cain haunts these very woods. You saw him in the paper five years ago. He had to gnaw his own arm off to free it from the tree that had fallen upon it." She paused to look deeply at Mark. If it wasn't for his injuries, she wouldn't have brought the story up. "His friends had left him to die, and he went mad. Revenge was all he craved, and he sought it out. He burned down the cabin after tying up his five friends, not to mention his girlfriend." She stopped to look at Mary. My heart stopped briefly but when Mark squeezed, it pumped again.

"His guilt took him deep in the woods. He stood above his dismembered arm and laughed. That laugh took him to hell when he pulled the trigger." I shut my eyes and buried myself in Mark. His grip tightened, and Stephanie grinned. "Steven remains in these woods, along with his friends. You can hear his laugh at night—and the screams of the burning. They all made it into hell with open arms. All of them had betrayed those close to them." I could feel tears in my eyes. She was smarter than she appeared.

Mark looked at me and used his left hand to catch a tear. He leaned in close to whisper. "I won't let them get you." My smile grew, and I gave him a hug. As much as it, hurt something in me was cracking, allowing me to leave behind the fear of affection.

"Why don't you tell us a story, Valencia?" Tiffany had spoken softly.

Every fiber in me was against the thought, but I stood anyway. All eyes were on me and I tucked my wings in deeper, even though I had to strain.

"Where I come from, we have stories of angels and demons. One of the scariest is about angels. Angels are supposed to be the nicest, but there are bad ones. Just last week, one escaped from jail. She was cursed for betraying God. She fell to earth, and her wings turned black. Her halo burned to ashes, and she began to crave human blood." I caught Mark's eyes; he was listening closely. The others were eyeing me with a look to determine whether I was crazy. "The woods became her home, so she wouldn't be killed in any place more public. It was in the woods she found a demon. He was housing lost campers. Demons can have kind hearts, but they're quicker to rely on violence if threatened. He had killed in front of her and taught her how."

My eyes scanned the audience. Some had perked up, but the rest remained lifeless.

"He knew her father. The angel still couldn't trust him. Her father wants her dead. Her father is a full demon, eager to please Lucifer. He had killed many, and she never once wanted a part of his life. Now she has no choice but to obey and feed off of the campers. She has killed many in order to live, but her father wasn't happy. Instead of waiting for approval, she killed him with an arrow, and next to him fell the demon who took her in. She had fully turned, and now follows the scent of blood to continue living in the human world." I sat down quickly. My cheeks were on fire, and all the kids were looking at me. Mark squeezed my hand, telling me he liked the story, and that it would make the others think before bed.

I didn't smile but cooked another marshmallow instead. We all sat in silence after that before everyone slowly retreated into the house to change. I put on flannel pants and T-shirt when I was permitted to go into the bathroom. Mark found me before I entered the tent, and he told me good night. His kiss on my cheek left it burning. I smiled in response and went to the red tent.

All the girls had a sleeping bag set up. I just smiled and collapsed onto the empty space. The twins slept next to each other in matching pink bags. Mary had a green bag, and Stephanie had the purple one closest to me. As they came in, they all turned to me.

We stayed up, talking, and they had asked me if I liked Mark. When I responded with a *yes*, all but Mary were happy. That night, once they stopped talking and went to sleep I snuck out of the tent. I walked into the woods and turned at the footsteps. Mark had followed me; he had heard me leave.

"You can sleep in the house if you want, or you can go home." I shook my head and walked up to him.

"I sleep better after a run." As I turned to go, he joined my side, wanting to run with me. My lips curled into a big smile.

"You don't have to come, Mark, you look tired."

He smiled and chuckled softly. "I can't leave you in the woods alone—I promised I wouldn't let anything get to you." My heart warmed, and I gave him a kiss on the cheek. He blushed and reached for my hand.

"I'll go sleep in the house. You can keep it safe with the doors locked." We turned and walked back to the cabin. It was dark as we entered. He flipped a switch to illuminate our path. We walked to the girl's room. Inside were two queen-sized beds and a master bathroom. I smiled and walked up to one of the beds. It was soft, with two pillows.

After I had crawled in he went in on the other side. He didn't get under the covers. My heart was beating at a new level, and my breathing quickened. He sat up next to me, but lowered himself a little more. Reaching over himself, he pulled me closer. I flinched away, causing him to stop.

"I'm sorry, I'm not used to this." He smiled softly and scooted away, just enough to prove he'd give me space if I asked directly. "Valencia, we don't have to do anything. I was just going to hold you until you sleep."

My eyes looked away, and my heart melted. This was it was like to be with a human—they seemed to care even more. With a small nod, I moved next to him. He took off the sling and used that arm to pull me to him. My head rested on his chest so I could listen to his heartbeat. Fingers slid through my hair.

"You're something special, Mark. Be here when I wake, promise me." My voice was muffled and faint, but I heard him promise before I slipped unconscious.

CHAPTER 14

I awoke to soft snores and a warm presence. He had kept his promise. Trying hard not to wake him, I slipped under his arm. His fingers grasped my shoulder, and he sat up, pin straight. Faintly I heard his whisper: "Don't go." I continued to move, promising to return quickly. As fast as I could, I left the room. If my shell hadn't been broken by now, then nothing had happened in the room.

I tiptoed into the kitchen. Looking out the window, I saw that everyone was asleep still. My smile grew, and I opened the fridge. There was microwavable bacon and eggs. Following the instructions, I soaked a paper towel and placed several slices of bacon on it. It landed on a plate with ease and went in the microwave.

The eggs came out scrambled right when the timer rang. I separated the food evenly among two dishes. A fork sat in each lump of egg as I walked back to Mark. He had started to sit up, and his face brightened when he saw me. Joining his side once more, I set his plate on his lap.

"Breakfast in bed?" He was astonished when I nodded. After several bites, I looked at him. "You are different, Valencia."

The fire returned to my cheeks. "If you only knew." I muttered low, hoping he wouldn't hear.

When his fork stopped moving the worse had been revealed. "What makes you different?"

I ate the last slice of bacon and went to stand up. "No one is the same." I left the room and went to wash all the dishes. No one else had awoken yet. Ten minutes passed before he joined my side.

He started to help me after complimenting my food. "Valencia, you can tell me anything." I shook my head but his fingers found my chin. He turned my face to look at him. His eyes sparkled in concern and care. His lips found mine and held on for a moment. "No one but us will know."

I bit my lip but nodded. "Promise you will tell no one, not even the slightest hint, Mark." He promised, and I continued to wash the dishes. He moved closer, and my brain swirled, screaming it was time. Releasing the pain in my back, I extended my right wing and wrapped it around him. His hand dropped down and touched the inner feathers. He ran his hand along them for a moment, taking it in.

"You're the girl from the story." That's when I smelled the blood under his skin. I quickly drew the wings back in as if they were never there.

"No, I took my story and twisted it into a horror. I have never killed, and I never betrayed God. I was framed. If you utter a word, I have a bow at home with plenty of arrows."

He understood the message clearly. "Will you tell me the whole story when we are alone?" I nodded and finished the last dish. He kissed my cheek once more before I went to get dressed. Jeans and a tank top went on with a small jacket.

Mark had waited for me in the kitchen. He came up to me to give me a hug and compliment my outfit as the others appeared and nearly keeled over looking into the now-clean sink on their way to the fridge.

"We were talking, and we all decided we want to go down to the diner for lunch tomorrow. I would like you to join us and visit tonight." Mark said.

I smiled and agreed.

After thanking everyone and saying good-bye, I grabbed my bag and left. Mark followed quickly to walk me home. When we got close to where I left him yesterday, Virnant drove up. I giggled and turned to Mark as the window rolled down.

"I'm hoping you treated her nicely this time." His voice was stern, but I saw it as an act. Mark responded with respect and mentioned the future plans. Virnant agreed, and I got in the car after Mark kissed me again. We sped off, leaving him there.

"Since when did you like boys?"

I blushed at the comment. "He found me in the woods and took me inside. He stayed with me until I slept. Oh and he knows I have wings . . ." I slipped the last part in a small voice, but the car stopped immediately.

"Valencia, what did you do?"

My smile slipped and I looked away. "He told me I was different and promised not to tell. I touched him with a wing, and he didn't freak out. Maybe he's the one."

The car drove again, and he laughed. "Be careful, while you're out I have an errand to run so I'll pick you up on the way." With that we arrived home. I showered and unpacked as Virnant made a call or two.

CHAPTER 15

I changed into better looking jeans and a nice green shirt with an open back, and Virnant had made a pizza when he was on the phone. What we didn't eat went into the fridge. He had me practice a few moves on the ground—our training had started again.

I'd throw a punch, and he'd block before doing the same. The kicks were easier to place and harder to block. We had worked for a few hours before downing bottles of water. Virnant wanted to warn me about something, but kept quiet. He gave me a hug before I flew off.

My hair didn't get in my face as my wings carried me to Mark. I did a few loops in the air before landing a good distance from his cabin. Halfway there, Mark met me coming up the driveway. He gave me a hug, and I let my wings wrap around him. His grip tightened a little to show he was nervous. I pulled my wings back and had them dig in close.

"They made a dinner, and I saved you a plate. We can walk after eating." He took my hand and led me into the house. Stephanie was waiting in the kitchen, and the others were watching TV. The dinner he had mentioned was a burger for each of us. He had waited to eat with me.

Stephanie hugged me and hung out with us as we ate. She was happy about something that I didn't know. She sat close to me and I could smell the bittersweet copper under her skin. My jaw clenched after the last bite. The meat and cheese were gone. Mark finished and took me outside. The rest stayed in the cabin.

Our fingers intertwined as we headed into the woods. When we were at the creek again, I let my wings relax and come out. It hurt to keep them that close. He stayed near, getting used to the feel of them.

The edges had started to fray on the bottom feathers; the curse was spreading.

It was only minutes of silence before his lips met mine. His arm pulled me closer, and I allowed it. We didn't part—only got closer. All my comfort levels were setting alarms off, but nothing stopped my actions. He was the one who pulled away. With a smile, he tucked me under his arm as best he could. My head rested on his shoulder, and my wing held him tighter.

"We can stay here all night, Valencia. Will you tell your story?" My shell had crumbled.

"I was born in Heaven with white wings. My mother is an angel, and my father is a demon. I have six older siblings who are all demons. If I had black wings, then father wouldn't have given me up. Mother left to find a human. She always liked humans, and I never knew why." I looked into his eyes and gave him a small kiss. "I was given to his younger sister. She was a mother to me. When she was young, she had her wings dyed white, because she wanted to be angelic. We both earned our halos. There's one big difference, though—I've always been innocent until I came here, or was forced. I don't mean 'no sex,' but no male touch of any kind, unless it was a friend hugging me good-bye, but only if he was an angel."

Mark looked at me and kissed my forehead. "I'm lucky then aren't I?"

I giggled and nodded my head. "Only guy I liked more than a friend. Anyway, word spread to Hell also. My father has been determined to impress Lucifer, so he created a rumor I betrayed God and was feeding secrets to Lucifer. Someone paid off a group of guys to not only rough me up so I looked like I visited it there often, but to testify. The court believed them instantly. While I was in the holding cell, I received word from Lucifer. He offered to break me out and protect me if I married him. He's the demon of all demons, so the thought repulsed me. Then Audrey was kidnapped, but I'm sure she escaped or was freed. I had managed to escape and come here."

His eyes grew and I went silent for a moment. He urged me to continue. When I didn't respond right away he gave me another kiss. This one was deeper.

"My whole family saw me leave. Mother had returned with a human boy, and father was angry when he heard I wouldn't accept.

I was found guilty by the third trial. Punishment for betrayal is a horrid curse or wings clipped, and the lucky ones get both. My halo burned, and my wings turned black. All my powers are gone, and I've started the worst phase." Tears streamed my face and he held me closer. His lips met each one so they'd disappear. He truly cared, even though I was becoming a monster.

"The shadows followed me, but I lost them. Virnant found me; he knew my father. He was banned from my life, though, until I fell. If the shadows catch me, they can either drag me to Hell for worse punishment or kill me on the spot." I felt Mark tremble this time. My wing pulled him closer. The smell of blood only tempted me more. My jaw clenched shut, and my head lowered to my knees.

"What's the phase you're in, Valencia?"

His calming voice made me utter the word, "Blood." He pulled away, and I drew my wings in. I had frightened him. There was nothing he could say to ease the tension. I stood and got into a running stance.

His hand grabbed my wrist before I could start. "You have shared secrets with me you can't tell anyone else. I can see that you trust me. In order to thank you, I offer my blood." My eyes met his, and I sat down again. He reached into his pocket and pulled out a small knife, which was attached to other useful objects. He made a small cut on his wrist, avoiding the major veins. Blood trickled out as he held his arm out to me. "Valencia, you need it. Once you take some we'll be closer. I'll stop you when it hurts."

Against my will, I gave a nod and pounced. My mouth encircled the wound, and I began to drink. Hands grabbed his wrist to hold it closer. The warmth flowed over my tongue and eased the gnawing of my brain. He kept a tight fist for a while. It was when he gave a soft groan that I pulled away. My fingers went to touch the wound, but they shook and dropped in my lap instead. "I used to be able to heal wounds. Thank you, Mark, this means everything to me." His response was a kiss.

When I stood this time, I snapped my wings out and lifted upward. Amazement was written on his face as I flew around just enough so he could see. I joined his side again, and we laid down to watch the stars. His hand held mine, and his other pointed out constellations.

He stole kisses often before I tucked my wings in tight. We snuggled close and fell asleep. This was a fairytale in the making.

I had nightmares though, and every time I woke, he sat up too; and every time, he eased me back down onto the grass and held me tighter. He meant everything he was doing. His concern was priceless and rewarded with kisses. The last nightmare ended with my death and woke me to the sun rising. After apologizing for giving him a restless night, he walked me to his cabin.

Virnant was waiting out back, worried sick. Stephanie had stayed up with him, and she looked exhausted. He eyed us over, but, with a stiff nod, he gave me a hug and left. Stephanie pushed us with questions before informing us she'd be staying home so she could sleep.

CHAPTER 16

The main phone was ringing, and Tiffany answered. Her face was puzzled, but she shrugged and went to get Stephanie, who ended up deciding to come along. Everyone else was headed out the door to get in the cars. The twins took their convertible, with Mary in the backseat. In the jeep were the two boys. Mark took me to the jeep and helped me up so I could sit in the back. He sat next to me, holding my hand.

Each engine revved to life. The convertible had started to pull out just when Stephanie appeared. She hopped in with the girls after waving to me. Spencer drove off, wanting to eat. The cars went smoothly along the winding road. We passed my cabin and took a left.

I could hear music from the girls' car. Mark caught the look in my eyes and leaned forward to turn the radio up. Surely he had to be the one. The song that came up was "Love Me Tender" by Elvis. He was a big hit in Heaven. The two guys up front made faces and laughed when Mark and I got closer.

The woods faded behind us as a town came into view. There were shops and markets. We had passed two fast-food joints before we turned into a parking lot. In front stood the classic model of a diner. The lights were off, but there were enough people inside.

The girls parked next to us and got out, smiling and dancing. We went in and got the round booth in the back. The booth was red leather, along with the stools at the counter. On the counter was a TV playing the news. Mark kept an arm around me as we ordered.

The waitress went back to the cook with a variety of requests for toasts, eggs, and bacons. Stephanie didn't order anything. She sat, watching the news, but occasionally glancing at me as if I'd vanish.

Everyone talked, but no one understood a word. The other customers were getting up to leave.

Just as the first one got to the door, an alarm went off on the TV. Stephanie's eyes sparkled as a dark-haired woman on the screen sat up with perfect posture. The alarms settled down so everyone could hear the voice clearly. We all by now had turned and stopped to watch. My best guess was that this didn't happen often.

"I am Jane Weatherspoon, and we just got reports on a missing girl. She was seen out in the camping area where she originally vanished. Later today, her family will be here with a photo and a clear description. For now all we know, is she is young, dangerous, and has brown hair. If you see anyone with the description, you are advised to contact the police at this number." Blue digits rolled across screen, and eyes turned to me.

Instantly my hands shot up in defense. "It ain't me; my father abandoned me when I was little, and I'm staying with my uncle. If I was missing, wouldn't my uncle tell my father where I was?" They all nodded and turned away when the food came. Stephanie sat still, watching us all eat. I had gotten a smiley face on my plate.

I ate slowly, my heart pounding. The news report had to be on someone else. My luck was running dry just as quickly as my plate emptied. Stephanie took a slice of my bacon and gave a slight wink.

"Valencia, did you want to stay with us and watch the news to see who the girl is?" Tiffany had spoken directly to me. With a smile, I agreed. At least if I watched it there, I'd have a better chance at running off. I would be outnumbered greatly, but they were still human. I would never be human.

Like gentlemen, the boys paid, and we all stumbled back outside. It was an overcast day, but the girls wanted to go shopping anyway. We loaded into the cars and headed out farther. Tom drove this time leading us to a large plaza full of clothing stores. The giddy girls went wild into the shops. Stephanie stayed on the side of me that Mark wasn't on.

Tom and Spencer went into the sports store. I told Mark he could go, but he opted to stay with me. Stephanie didn't leave us for a moment. Even with her there, he managed to steal a few kisses. He had the radio on, and we swayed to the soft tune as Stephanie danced. We began to clap, and she moved faster and twirled more.

Her hair swayed perfectly, never getting in her face. She had on a skirt, so it twisted with every movement.

When the others came out, Stephanie was begging to get home quick to see the news. Their curiosity had risen as they had shopped, making us rush out of there. Stephanie squeezed into the back of the jeep with us. There was enough room for her to do so.

We went up the winding road once more, just slower. Just as we got there, Virnant stepped out in front of the car, making us halt immediately. He agreed to let me go with the others—if I came right home afterward. Stephanie promised I'd be returned shortly. His chuckle filled the tension, and he went back up the driveway. I shook my head slightly as the car began to move again.

Outside the second cabin was a news truck. We all assumed it was the family of the girl. The car putted onward and up to the teens' place. Everyone piled around or on the couch instantly. Mark and I sat next to it, our hands practically glued together.

The TV blinked on, and Stephanie stood off to the side, closer to the door. Channels flashed by until we found Jane again. She was standing in front of a wooden door, talking into a microphone, claiming this to be Channel 5.

"Earlier today, I had told you there was a missing girl. I am now with the family who are staying in the woods, looking for her." The woman knocked on the door, and it opened.

CHAPTER 17

M y jaw fell, and I had no words. I was looking at my father. His curls were neater and brighter, as if he got his hair done from someone other than himself. He was wearing dark clothes, as if mourning. He was sitting on a couch, his arm stretched back. The camera zoomed into the five kids with him. My heart escalated when I couldn't find the other. All of them had a variety of black and brown hair that was straight or curly. Jane sat down across from everyone, and Father took the other seat.

"I am Jane Weatherspoon, and I would like to talk to you about your missing daughter. Do you have a photo we can use?" He reached around himself and lifted up a medium-sized square of paper. On it was my picture. It was of me flying in the woods, except my wings were cut out. Heads spun to look at me as my father stared deep into the camera. His cold dark eyes ran over me.

"All I want is my daughter Valencia back. She ran off when we came here, because she doesn't like the outdoors. She's a troubled young girl who can hurt you if you threaten her. We had tried to keep her home-schooled so not many would see her, but now we know that, if her face isn't out there, we won't get her back." He looked pained, but I knew him very well; it was all an act, so someone would take me to him. Stephanie started laughing and locked the door. Mark held me tighter, as if he knew it was lies. Mary stood up and walked over to me.

"You lied to us. I'm calling that number. Spencer, go drive there and see if they can pick her up." She went to the phone, and tears ran down my cheeks. I gave Mark a kiss and made a mad dash to the back door. Stephanie was quicker, she grabbed my arm to make me go still. I spun to get in a punch, but she ducked and tackled me.

Father's voice filled the cabin as Stephanie dragged me to the girl's room. Mark followed me in, promising he'd find me a way out, but his face was skeptical.

I said to him, "It's okay, you don't have to fight for me. It'll only end in you getting hurt."

He gave me a hug, and I went to the window. Tina appeared on the other side. My fist hit the wall, and my breathing got heavier. Mark had gone out the door already. Stephanie came in, and she smirked. Her eyes glanced at the window, but Tina had already turned around to watch for the sign of cars coming. I looked at the girl in front of me, and she began to shimmer and vibrate. After a minute, she turned into my eldest sister.

I nearly shrieked, but instead I was frozen still. "Annilia, what are you doing here?" I finally found my sixth sibling.

"Father needs you, so I made friends, and they think they know me. My powers still work." Her last sentence was a low blow. I sat on the bed. I shook my head and then sighed. She had been there when I needed her, and now she had switched sides. "If you obey, you'll get your powers back—and Mark. We could bring him with us." My eyes bugged at the thought. That would be the one thing they could use against me to get me to do anything they wanted. I heard cars pull in, and my faith shattered.

"Where's Audrey?"

I lowered my head a little, but Annilia answered. "She was killed yesterday. We mistook her when we were hunting. She had come to look for you, but we intercepted first."

My heart shattered, and the front door opened. If I didn't hurt so badly, I would have stood up. I could only manage a sitting position. Father came into the bedroom on my right side. His long curls hung down as he leaned over me.

"Hello, Valencia. we're here to take you home now."

Virnant flashed into my head and I swung a fist at Father. His hand caught it instantly and squeezed just to bend it backward.

"There will be none of that." The pain sent down my arm was enough. I started to stand but instead went down to attack. His hand lifted me and threw me onto the bed. I landed on my stomach. He snapped at one of the boys, who then came up to me. I didn't dare move. I looked up to see Augustus; he was named after Caesar's son. Father always dreamt of being king.

His hands grabbed my wrists and pulled them behind my back. He pulled out a mangled rope and began tying, not caring that it had already started to cut into my skin. After a minute, he pulled me to my feet. I stood, staring at his black hair. It was shorter than when I saw him. To my shock, it was a buzz cut. His emerald eyes only filled with excitement. I was lifted and thrown over his shoulder, which dug deep into my stomach.

"Put me down! I can walk, my legs aren't broken!" My voice was muffled at this angle, but it was heard just enough for me to get gagged next. Out of habit, my legs thrashed, and his grip pushed his shoulder in more. I stopped instantly from the pain.

Father stopped to thank everyone, and my eyes caught Mark's. He ran to me, making my brother pause. His offer to carry me was denied. The walking started up again, and I was placed into a large SUV; It had to be black. Mark got in next to me and refused to leave. Father's eyes twinkled, and he shut and locked the door. Mark held me close as the others piled in around us. Father drove, and Annilia flew, because her seat was taken.

"You've caused us great pain, Valencia." My father's words echoed in the car. I rested my head on Mark.

The car ride was silent from then. We pulled up to their cabin, and Annilia was already waiting for us. Her smirk said it all as I was taken out of the car. Mark followed obediently when no one said anything. He was free to run until he was in the house. I was tossed on the couch. Mark came quick and untied my mouth. I leaned forward and released my wings. Each feather shook itself and rested back down. The left wing wrapped around him, and my father was mortified.

"You exposed yourself to a human." I had to strain very hard not to comment about mother. That would only enrage him. "What is your name and business with my daughter?" Mark's eyes widened and looked up at him. All the children studied him, except Annilia.

"I am Mark, and I happen to love your daughter." My heart beat faster, and my wing pulled him closer. I still had rope slicing at my wrists. Every single face was in awe. Annilia giggled, and Father stepped closer.

He didn't find any of this amusing. "What have you done with her?"

Mark's eyebrow raised, and I gave a little smile. "Still the innocent one, Father."

His nod was enough to show he understood. He walked away and into a room. Mark looked over my siblings, and I started to stand.

"Can one of you untie me so I can introduce you all to him?" Annilia moved first. She came quick and pulled at the ends. It came undone easily. My hands ran over each wrist, counting every wound. I turned to Mark. "I'm only saying this once, and they're born in the order I'm going to say." As if on cue, they all lined up.

I sucked in a deep breath so I could spit out each name in one go. "Augustus, Annilia, Beatrice, Cornelius, Deidra, and Ezekiel."

They all stood, tall and proud, and then Mark laughed. "You are alphabetical? Why isn't Valencia?"

I lowered my eyes. "I was the odd child plus the seventh, which is some special number to my father." I went to sit again as he came out of the room.

He had heard what I said. "Now you get to be the lucky child."

My head shook, and I curled up next to Mark.

CHAPTER 18

I was sent to bed without dinner. It was like being punished when I was little. Mark was sent to sleep right in the living room where Augustus would watch over him. I had to sleep with the other kids so I was completely surrounded. I didn't even get the bed. I was set up in the tub which turned out to be comfy. Father had his own room that none of us were allowed in.

As soft as the blankets were I couldn't sleep. I tossed and turned all night which was difficult in the tight space. I was just lucky no one turned the water on when Deidra came to get me. We went to the kitchen where Mark was eating cereal. I wasn't offered anything when I sat across from him.

Father came out, so the others had to be out too. Virnant even came over. My head hit the table and stayed there. When he came closer, he was holding a bag. It dropped next to my feet. Mark only stared.

"You were supposed to be on my side."

Virnant laughed, and Father patted his back in that common-guy way. "And you were supposed to obey and train with me. Don't forget that affectionate touches used to frighten you."

I let my eyes close. Mark's hand patted my head. He had finished eating.

Cornelius spoke in an even tone. "Father, let's just kill them. He knows who we are and what we are and she has brought shame upon us." His words darkened the room, but I didn't raise my head any. My stomach was growling, which filled the silence.

"No, she's our ticket. If she is dead, we will get nothing." His voice was filled with venom. I began to stand, but Ezekiel held my shoulders down so only my head lifted.

"Your ticket to what?"

Mark went to put his bowl in the sink.

"Remember your proposal from Lucifer? It's still in play, and, if we take you there in the next seventy-two hours, then the shadows will not return. Not only will you be safe, but we can all live in the castle."

My eyes met Mark's. He had admitted to loving me and here I was being sold off. "What about my wings? Or Mark? We can't bring him, and if we could, he'd be killed after I was married off."

My youngest brother lowered his head to whisper. "It's him or the wings."

My eyes twinkled. "Then I choose him. You can have these stupid wings. None of you can get into Hell without me." I fought until I was standing. Mark stood by my side and took my hand. He had no clue the choice I had made. If you lost your wings, you wouldn't live, depending on how much they clip. They can cut off enough to keep you from flying but if they were shaved, you died.

Father walked up to us, and I stood tall. All eyes were on us. His actions were limited, but unpredictable. I waited for him to strike, but he just grabbed my chin. He pulled me away from Mark, but our hands remained together. "You will never disrespect your family again. Valencia, you will obey me. If this human means so much to you, then you will have one final night with him. Only if your husband allows it can you visit. I doubt you will ever see him again, but do not, and I repeat, do not even attempt to have sex. He likes your innocence best, and if it is gone, you will die unloved, and this human will join you." I deciphered his message and gave him a hug. Father had finally done something that wasn't for himself only. I would be able to spend time with Mark. I released my father and started to take Mark out the back door.

Annilia stopped us. Since we weren't allowed out, she offered to make us more lasagna. All the other siblings left to fly and hunt. Virnant and Father went outside to talk. Mark and I cuddled on the couch and watched a movie. He called it the *Titanic*.

Father's dark eyes constantly looked through the window. I felt annoyed, so when I caught him, I kissed Mark, who didn't object until the door burst open. I just smiled while Mark shuddered.

"Valencia, do you want him to live?"

My smirk grew as he stepped in. Virnant leaned in to see the action. Even Annilia stopped to peek in.

"You said no sex, it was only a kiss. Shouldn't I be practicing to please my husband?"

He grunted but went to his room. Virnant said good-bye and flew off.

"Do you still need blood?" Mark whispered so low so only I could hear.

"I've been trying to ignore the smell. Do you still have the knife?"

With a nod he reached into his pocket. He made a new slice and gave me his wrist. His smile said it all as I began to feed. He held me closer until I finished.

"I love you, Mark."

The bedroom door opened, and his eyes twinkled. I pulled him closer and wrapped my wings around us to hide. He gave me a kiss, and then the wings securing us were torn open. Father was glaring down at us, He pulled me by my wings and put me in my room. I was thrown against the wall.

"I will never hear you say that to a *human* ever again. They are nothing in this world. You are going to be a great something."

I just nodded under his harsh words and went back to Mark. It wasn't easy trying to stay calm, but I survived until dinner.

CHAPTER 19

The dinner was only Mark and me, making it special. Annilia went outside to watch the sun drop. Father went to see Virnant. I made Mark rush, and we escaped out the front door. We had a small window of opportunity, and we seized it. My wings still ached, but I took his hand and flew us up. We landed on the roof. It could have been better, but we were together.

The moon came up, and the sky darkened so we could see stars again. We held each other tight, occasionally stealing kisses. It was within that time that I wanted to wreck my father's dreams. He had crushed every dream of mine, and I know he took Audrey. This would end everything for him.

I started to kiss Mark deeper, not moving away. He didn't object. It was when my fingers had started to unzip his jacket that he moved away. His eyes were worried, but I still shrunk back.

"Valencia, are you sure? This means death." I looked him over. He was scared—not for just him, but for me. My heart was melting, and it belonged to him.

"We would be the only ones to know until the honeymoon. Plus we love each other, and you are the first guy who ever meant this much to me."

He smiled and kissed me again. I had gotten my answer from him.

We didn't get to enjoy our night. Father found us. Mark's jacket was somewhere else but on him. The front of my shirt was torn at the top. I was lifted by my wings. Mark was left there as I crashed to the ground. My head hit the car, and I rolled off onto pavement. I shrieked and little faces started to swirl into my view. It was Beatrice who brought Mark down.

"Valencia, I told you before not to even attempt it—not to mention you were outside the house with no one watching you. I will be back in ten minutes, and if I am not calmer or didn't get a response, your wings will be clipped. Can you understand that?"

My head nodded against the pain. Father walked away, and Mark came over sitting close to me. I squeezed his hand and tried to sit up. I saw stars instead. With groans, I pushed myself to my knees. He tried to hold me, but I kept pushing him back. I needed to do this on my own.

Ezekiel, being himself, came over and lifted Mark up. I forced my eyes to work and look at them. He didn't throw a punch or attack; he just placed him on the hood of the car. I sat back on my legs, trying to catch my bearings. All I could feel was blood in my mouth. Spitting and gagging were my only options. When I had relieved my mouth of the copper taste, I pushed hard. Using my wings for support, I stood up. I heard a clap and turned to see Virnant. My vision was still blurred. On his shoulder was my bow.

"For being strong, I give you an early wedding present." He handed me Audrey's bow and her arrows. I just nodded. He would be joining us too, because he was on their side. My eyes ran over his expression; he was amused.

Father walked out and saw the bow. His dark eyes looked me over. I just stared at him. He had his hands behind his back. Quickly his attention moved to Mark. As he walked closer, he turned so I couldn't see behind him. His steps took him right up to Mark. With a nod, Ezekiel stepped away from the car and to me. Mark was taken to the door but not inside. Father wanted him to see what would happen.

Chapter 20

All eyes rested on Father. No one was breathing. I was holding my breath, fearing he held a weapon to clip my wings. His dark curls bobbed as he twisted, pulling around a black box. Relief rushed through me, seeing that I would keep my wings, but a new worry settled in.

"You are my youngest child, Valencia, and I dream the best for you. I underestimated you, and now I see the errors of my way. This came for you when I was with Virnant." He opened the box, and resting on top was a letter. The paper was signed with red-and-black streaks. It was folded into a little square. Father pulled it into the top of the box to show me it would be read later. Underneath it was a ring. It wasn't just a ring—it was *the* ring. Lucifer's favorite ring was sitting in front of me with a new design.

Originally it was just black wings made of burned bones that wrapped around your finger, each bone carved and cut perfectly to represent feathers. What connected the wings on top was a large, black diamond. It shined even in the moonlight. It was changed so that the center of the diamond was carved out to fit a bright-red, heart-shaped ruby. On the ruby were an *L* and a *V* in looped letters.

My eyes grew, and Father motioned Augustus over. Handing him the box, he removed the ring. Without a word he took my hand and placed the ring on it. Mark's pain radiated to me, and the tears welled up. It hurt to watch my finger wear a symbol so great. Father smiled and took out the letter. He opened it slowly and began to read. I could smell the blood it was written in—the poor soul had been tortured before he was bled. The smell of pain still lingered.

"To my dearest Valencia, this gift is a token of my lust for you. The wedding has been planned and will be ready in the same week you arrive. Every dream you ever have will be granted after the ceremony. I can make your world perfect. Forever, Lucifer."

Father stood, grinning, and the others clapped. Mark walked into the house. I shook my wings and stretched them out. Father nodded, and I took to the sky. Ten minutes of flying blind from the tears passed. It was Deidra who found me. She flew upside down so she could talk to me.

"Why aren't you happy? You finally get to live a fairytale life in a real castle." My wings beat down hard, causing her to drop at least ten feet while I went up twenty. All I wanted was to be alone. Every time I talked to someone, they were on a different side. They all wanted the same thing; they wanted to keep my father pleased.

It was then that everything struck me. Evan had such great power over his children. He had every single one of them living with him in his house on Earth. If he didn't approve of something, it was forbidden with deadly consequences. Breathing was a privilege in his eyes; he would be the one to take it away if you disobeyed. Inside, we were all terrified of him.

Deidra took the hint and flew off. She went back to the cabin, and I flew higher. I was headed toward the moon when I blacked out. It was awhile before I came to. My head was pounding, and I couldn't move my arms. Everything began thrashing as I opened my eyes.

Mark was looking down at me. I smiled and reached for a kiss, but when our lips met, a horrible shock was emitted through the ring. It was my scream that woke my father. He came out and smirked down at me. I went to sit up on the couch when I noticed my hands were tied down. Just what I needed—more cuts on my arms.

"You're awake. Deidra said you were trying to escape."

I shook my head. She always loved getting others in trouble. It had to be her talent. "No, I wanted to get closer to the moon. Can you untie me?" Mark had moved to the wall on the other side of the room. He understood the dangers my father brought to life. Father bent down and untied my left hand.

"If I untie the other one, will you go to bed and stay there until morning?" Something in me broke, making me laugh.

"Don't have a bed. They made me sleep in the tub last night." Anger flashed through his eyes. Silently, he stood and walked into my sisters' room. Mark came over and freed my other hand. He kissed my cheek this time so I wouldn't get electrocuted. I stood up, and he sat down. Out stumbled six half-awake kids, and they went out the door. Father walked over and kissed my head, telling me to go to sleep.

I did as told and crawled into the bed. It was softer than the one at Virnant's. Sleep was disrupted by a dream, where I was back with Audrey. We were in her big, white house with a million rooms that we'd run around in when I was little. For hours we'd play hide 'n' seek. If it rained, we'd have tea parties.

When I awoke, I had a smile. I looked out the French doors and saw the bright sun hanging onto the trees. Hopping up from the bed, I went to take a shower. It was when I came out of the bathroom that I saw a dress on the bed. It was completely black with a ruffled bottom. Thankfully, it had thick straps. I took the hint and put it on. My hair was still soaked when I left the room. Father was waiting; he had breakfast ready. Mark was still asleep.

"Good morning, princess, how did you rest?" I sat at the table. He had made pancakes with bacon. There was syrup and butter dripping off the edges.

"Better than last night." He sat across from me as I ate. I kept my head down. If I could, I would be out that door with Mark, where they couldn't find us.

"Today we will go drop Mark off, and then I will get to show you the castle." I had two pancakes left and a slice of bacon drowning in syrup. My fork rested on the edge of the plate.

"Can we bring him with us? You said if Lucifer was okay with it, I could still visit him."

Father's eyes bugged out of his head. I looked down and continued to eat again. "He could die, Valencia. Do you want to risk that?"

My eyes fell on my father's. I finished chewing the wonderful breakfast. "There's a chance I could cut my wings if he does." I had a blank face and steady voice as I spoke. It was proof I was nothing like what he left behind. There would be no games with me.

"That will bring shame on our family."

I laughed, but made sure I didn't laugh too loudly. "You shamed us all by giving your daughter away, you killed your sister, and you can't even keep a wife!" He leaned over the table and slapped me. As my cheek changed colors and stung, Father stood, taking my plate. I stayed where I was with my eyes shut. The plate clanged next to the sink. His door slammed, and Mark awoke. He came to me, but I pushed him away.

Chapter 21

All my siblings, along with Virnant, showed up, dressed in their best. Father came out of his room, dressed in a suit. We piled into three cars, and I got to ride with Mark. He fought to stay with us to the end. If I didn't ache all over, I would have swooned at how much he cared.

Thankfully, Father rode in the other car. His was the first one, and Virnant's was the last. Annilia and Augustus drove Mark and me in the middle car to ensure I couldn't escape. I did have the heels back, which brightened the trip, reminding me of that night with Mark.

We pulled up to a graveyard and stepped out of the cars. Mark stood next to me, utterly confused. Father took the lead and marched to a mausoleum while the rest of us followed. He snuck in, and we all went in and down the stairs. He knocked on the wall, and it opened to a blinding orange light. Mark took my hand as we all shuffled inside.

Everything spun as we fell. My head ached on the way down. Mark's hand was squishing mine. I heard laughter, and then a crackling. My feet hit a soft ground, and Mark quickly released me. I let my eyes flicker open until I was staring at a group of dark shadows standing all around us. My heart and breathing stopped completely.

Father walked up to the group and lifted my hand. The ring dazzled, and the group opened to let us through. We all moved forward, and I looked around us. If we weren't in the castle, then the red-and-black stones surrounding us didn't exist. Father kept me by his side, and Mark was behind the three oldest children, but in front of everyone else.

We went up a set of stairs that winded up. It took us to a door that curved to a point at the top. It had a large knocker with a skull on it. Evan rapped it loudly. The door creaked open, and we all stood still. Inside were two men standing by a huge fireplace. The fires inside roared in brilliant colors. The rest of the room had windows bigger than the average human. There was a large desk with a throne-like chair and rows upon rows of books. It was such a lovely office—until I focused on the men.

One had glasses and fluffed brown hair. He had no eyes, but his suit was a navy blue. The other was *him*. I could tell from his expression. His horns poked above the black hair, and they shined as if freshly waxed. His tan skin was tinted red, most likely from killing. His dark eyes were huge, blocking out a lot of the white.

"You finally arrived. We have rooms waiting for everyone." He gave a slight nod to his partner as they walked closer. Father slithered away, leaving me alone up in front. Lucifer came closer and took my hand. He bent to kiss the ring he had given me. "It is nice to have you home, Valencia." All I could do was smile at him.

His partner had counted over the group before he spotted Mark, "There's an extra one." I turned instantly as all eyes set on him. "He's a human. Evan, why have you brought a human here?" Lucifer's voice shook the walls.

"Sir, this boy is my best friend, and I would like him to stay for the wedding." My voice was sturdy, and Mark's red cheeks started to return to a normal color.

"Will he return to Earth afterward?" The black eyes looking at me were fierce and meant business.

"Only if I am allowed to visit him." I could feel Father's eyes shoot daggers into my back.

"You may. Let us take a walk so I can show you the castle." His bent arm extended, and I set my hand on the inside of his elbow. As best I could, I looked happy. "Arthur, make sure he gets a very special room near hers so she feels at home." With that, we left. Everyone stayed put in the room until we had made it down the steps.

"So, my dear, what made you agree?" I looked away, unsure how to successfully answer.

"It took a few good hits from reality, along with being tied up in family matters to show me I needed someone as special as you to take me somewhere better in life." If anything, that was the best way I could put it without telling him flat-out that I had a loaded gun at every head that mattered to me, and it had already fired once.

"Now, Valencia, I hear you've lost your powers and already began craving for blood. I can restore you to your original self, but the wings remain black." I felt a smile creep on as we walked down a long hall with rooms on both sides.

"I would love that, sir." He gave a little chuckle and pointed ahead to two large double-doors painted red.

"That will be our room in a few days. You will be staying next to it in my special guest room. And please, call me Lucifer." He walked up to the small single red door. I just kept a smile on my face as he opened it. Inside was a large queen bed with an elegant gold-and-black quilt. There were two doors on the right so it wouldn't enter his room on the left. Straight ahead, past the bed, was an open balcony. It could fit four comfortably.

"This is lovely, Lucifer. I don't see how ours could be better."

It was his smile that gave it away but I ignored what he was hinting at. "After dinner I would like to walk you to your room and heal you. Will you be okay with that?" I nodded with a bright smile. It was with that nod I could feel every ache. It was amazing that the pain from yesterday and this morning waited so long to appear. Maybe I did change greatly from the curse.

CHAPTER 22

Lucifer took me everywhere but out of the castle. He showed me the dining hall and the kitchen. We even walked down to the area where those who worked here stayed. It was actually nice, even when I didn't get to see them. There were ballrooms and a library—even a secret passage around the castle. He never took me down to see the dungeon, though.

Our walk ended at the bottom of the stairs. He snapped, and a girl appeared. She had pin-straight blond hair and red eyes. Lucifer had her take me to my room and get me into a new dress. It was a lovely red gown to my ankles. The sleeves went halfway down from the elbow before it trailed down in red material. The neck was low in the front, but the necklace she put on ended in the center of my chest; it was a coffin with a pitchfork engraved on front.

Alias only spoke in a soft voice when she had to. She did my hair, leaving it half up. The heels she put on me tied up my legs, even though they wouldn't be seen. I had to ask for her not to put on makeup. That didn't settle well with her.

She didn't protest, but instead took me down to the dining hall. When I entered this time, there were more people crowding the long row. It was packed with food of all kinds. Every voice stopped so heads could look at me. I just smiled as she led me next to Lucifer. He sat at the head of the table, and I sat on his left. As I went to the chair next to his huge, handcrafted one, he rose and pulled my chair out.

"You look elegant, Valencia." I gave a nod and looked down to see my empty plate. He remained standing as he took his goblet and held it high. "Let's toast to Valencia. She has come to join me in marriage. May she have the time of her life." He raised his glass a little before taking a sip. It was wine. I did the same.

Lucifer sat and carved the chicken closest to him. He gave me the first slice. I reached to put mashed potatoes and corn on my plate. My head titled so I could look at my family scattered around the table. Mark sat at the other head. He looked distant, but he had on a dress shirt. Father was next to him, carving their own chicken.

My stomach growled, and I dug in. With every bite my jaw hurt. The pain from the slap finally hit hard. I'd probably get a bruise later. My plate emptied, and I looked at Lucifer. He had a mound of food on his. I added another serving of everything and included a roll this time.

There was talk everywhere, but I never said a word. If I said a word, the pain would crash down worse. Lucifer tried to tell me about the castle, but I only nodded. I was just glad he didn't discuss his work. That would just bore me. Father would discuss work when I was little; it'd put me to sleep.

"Valencia, we can retire early if you want. You can even take your friend to his room while I get a few things ready." With a smile and a nod, the three of us were soon going upstairs. I held the crook of Lucifer's arm, and Mark stayed close. Lucifer pointed to a blue door down the hall from mine, and then he turned into my room. I followed Mark as he opened his door and shut it quickly. His living space was similar to mine.

"Are you okay?" He eyed me over carefully.

"I'm fine. What's wrong? You look sad." I watched as he went up to his bed and sat down on the edge.

His head rolled but he looked up. "Hurts to see you with him, it drives me crazy."

My heart beat faster, and I walked closer. "I get to visit you, and I'll be all healed. So next time a tree falls on you, there will be no need for a doctor." We both laughed with lingering smiles. He stood and kissed my cheek. I gave him a hug. A knock on the door made us jump. We turned to watch Lucifer's head poke in. It was time to leave. Mark gestured for me to go so I did.

The dark eyes I walked toward brightened and led me down the hall to my room. As the door opened my nose met a wave of vanilla scented smoke; candles. I just smiled walking in more. He shut the door, and I turned to look at him.

"How is your friend?" I was lost with the question. He actually seemed to care.

"Mark's good, just lonely."

Lucifer offered to send him someone, but I knew better than to let him. "Well, tomorrow you two can walk the castle. For now, I get to heal you." His smile was bright, and he stepped closer. I stepped back slightly as his hand came up. His fingers took several misplaced hairs and pushed them back. "Relax, Valencia, everything will be okay." My jaw clenched tightly as his hand went up to my head. His palm pressed to the center, and the fingers relaxed. His free hand wrapped around me to pull me to him. I winced as my aches smashed into his built body. Lucifer didn't stop at the noise; he was too concentrated.

My brain went from busy and warm to basically mush. I was limp completely, forcing all my weight to slump against him. As my head rested on him, I never once, heard a heartbeat. Slowly the mush began to blow up like a beach ball. Heat flowed from his hand until I was standing, fully erect. He never said a word; he just removed his hands. The left arm went up and sliced itself on his horn. The arm dropped in between us, bleeding. His nonbloody hand wrapped lightly around my wrist, which he brought to his wound.

I let my fingers trace the cut. It was time to shine. As hard as I concentrated, the process was slow and irritated me. My cheeks flamed but, when the wound healed I only sighed. I was still broken.

"It will take time, and we can practice daily. Now tell me why it pained you when I held you." I let my eyes focus anywhere but his face.

"It's been a rough couple days. Injuries occur when you are trying survive." When my eyes did meet his, he knew I was lying about something. The glare he drew on his face made me go stock-still until the truth was practically bubbling out. "Last night father grabbed me by my wings in flight and threw me onto a car. I rolled onto the pavement, and he left me there. This morning he slapped me. They had kidnapped me and tied me. I didn't get food for a while." The anger that was in his face said it all. I had to act, and there were only a few ways I could think of.

My hands seized his shoulders. "Don't hurt him! He was thinking of the best for me, and I was fighting him every step of the way. I deserved what happened. Lucifer, thank you for restoring what you could." Leaning up, I kissed his cheek. I felt him relax beneath my grip.

He pulled me close and just held me. To my shock it was nice. "You should sleep. I will be here when you wake." His voice was soft in my ear. With that, he left the room, but the servant girl returned. She came in and blew out all the candles. I stayed where I was as she walked over to the first door. She was in there awhile. My head turned as she came out. In her hands was a nightgown. It was navy blue and long.

CHAPTER 23

Again we went through silence until I was finally under the covers. It was dark, but cozy. I was half-asleep when the door opened. I shot straight up. My eyes saw a flash of curls, and there was my sister Beatrice. She came closer and sat at the edge of my bed. I let my wings stretch out and then rest down.

"Valencia, I don't like this. Mark, he's depressed and won't leave his room. I had to practically force him to dinner." I relaxed a bit but stacked another pillow behind me so I was vertical.

"We can do nothing about any of this. Father has stuck us in this situation, and, if I disobey, Lucifer will have my head." We were whispering the whole time from fear of being caught.

"Annilia was supposed to be getting married, but then Father heard what Lucifer had said. She had to leave her fiancé to help get you here. He's dead now; he killed himself thinking she hated him. Let's take this chance to stick it to Father."

My fists were hidden under the covers. I shook my head, but I couldn't help but face the truth. Father had to go for everyone to live happy and free. "If we weren't in this very castle with that very demon in the next room, I'd gladly help you, but if I cross him, not only will I die, but Mark, you, and everyone else will. I already lost Audrey, and I haven't even had time to grieve about that." I could already feel the tears.

Beatrice leaned forward and gave me a big hug. We just held each other tight. In the end, we were still sisters. "Augustus has two children. Father doesn't know and Cornelius is engaged."

I had missed so much it was overwhelming. "What about you, is there someone in your life?" Her eyes dropped and looked away.

Nicole Brollier

She released me and moved back. It was like she was turning distant. "My name is Beatrice, after the girl in Dante's *Inferno*. She was taken by Lucifer. Father always hoped I'd be the one to get him. I never really was allowed out much. He wanted me to stay perfect. Only once did I sneak out, and I met a boy during that time. He wouldn't come back to meet Father."

I stayed where I was. If our roles were reversed, she would be sitting in this bed practically glowing, and I'd be down the hall either alone or with Mark. "You can have him if it means that much to you."

Her head shook, and she laughed. "Every night when Father would tuck us all in, he'd read to me the story. The only difference was he'd change out many parts so Lucifer was the one she deserved, and she loved him. I was twelve when I read the book on my own." It hurt just to hear that she had been raised to marry him. I knew it was worse for her. All her life she must have been dreaming of marrying the perfect guy her father selected, and here comes her abandoned sister stealing that guy. "You need sleep, there's a lot that's got to go on tomorrow before the wedding."

I let my eyes widen, and she gave me a hug. "When's the wedding, and do I get to pick anything?"

She laughed shaking her head. Her arms were tight around me. "He's picked everything and hired everyone to deal with everything. It's the day after tomorrow, so enjoy your day with Mark tomorrow. There won't be much you guys can do." Beatrice got up and left.

That morning, I awoke to Lucifer leaning over me, watching me sleep and pushing my hair to one side. He smiled as my eyes opened. Carefully, he pulled me upward as his other hand gathered pillows to put underneath me. I rested back, just looking him over. If I had known him better, I would be able to tell if he was thinking or just staring into space.

His hand raised and started to come toward me. Moments passed before it lifted and was cut on a horn. The arm rested on my lap, bleeding again. The red trickled down and stained the quilt. I let my fingers run over the cut. The healing was faster than last night, but not fast enough to satisfy me.

"Good morning, Valencia, did you sleep well?"

I smiled at him. He at least was trying to be nice. "Fine and did you?"

He shrugged it off and pulled me to my feet. We stood just inches apart, with him looking me over. His dark eyes were looking deep into mine.

"Tomorrow is our day. Are you ready?" My head tilted and eyes widened. "Ready to join me forever Valencia?" Knowing best, I just nodded. He kissed my cheek and left. The girl returned. She helped with today's outfit.

CHAPTER 24

Again I was placed in a dress, and thankfully, this was a sweater dress. It had long sleeves and came to my knees. It was gray but cozy soft. I was left alone in my room, so I went to the balcony. Outside it was warmer from all the red and orange colors of the sky. All I could see was woods and a graveyard. There was truly nothing but that and the garden space below. I was hoping it didn't look like this everywhere from every window.

A knock on my door made me spin. Mark walked in. He was back in his regular clothes. I smiled and rushed to him. He just held me in silence. There were no words to describe the feelings we felt anymore. Time was just slow, like slime from a snail.

"I get married tomorrow, but we have the whole day to ourselves."

As sad as his eyes were, he smiled. He lifted my hand and removed the ring. He set it on the bed right, in the center so I wouldn't miss it. This time when he kissed me, I wasn't zapped. Our rush of joy had us sliding around the room. As much as each wall stung, it was the fall to the ground that had me wince.

"Did I hurt you?" His breathless voice made me blush.

"No, just sore from hitting the car. Can we just go gentle? I don't need bruises."

I watched him nod and we stood up. "Valencia, I can't lose you." His voice was a whisper as he enclosed around me. My spine tingled as his fingers traced up my back. They stopped at the edge of the wings. He came closer, dropping his head. Lips trailed along my neck, and I pressed into him.

"I love you, Mark." As he came back up to my lips, he repeated my words.

We had managed to stay quiet so no one came in to check on us. The only thing that stopped us was a knock at the door. I shot away from him fast, and he went to hide on the balcony. The door opened to a young man. He had his hands behind his back, and he asked what I wanted for lunch. I tried to hide my surprise. Mark came around and walked up next to me. The boy didn't move; he just took our orders and walked away.

"That was close, now put on your ring, and we can talk by the balcony for when he returns." I followed his orders and joined his side. We stood, staring in silence.

Our lunch came on a tray. We sat on the bed with the sandwiches. If we had a menu at the time, it would have been something more elegant than ham. As we ate, we did get a chance to talk. It was his turn to tell me more about his life. It was when we finished that scared us most. The door opened, and Lucifer walked in. He eyed us carefully, but relaxed, seeing we weren't closer than a foot.

"Good evening, Mark. We have a tailor on his way to measure you for the suit. He will be down in the foyer. Valencia, your father wishes to see you, then your sisters have a surprise."

I smiled and began to stand. Mark gathered up the empty plates before I could. He left quickly, leaving me alone with my fiancé. Lucifer's arm extended for me to take his elbow yet again.

We walked up to his office. This time, Father was by the fire, looking in. He was in a dress shirt that was only half-buttoned. As he turned, his feet moved away from the flames. He gave me a hug, so I had to release Lucifer's arm.

"My darling daughter, I have something for you. As a tradition in my family, the first wife always gets this exact gift on the eve of her wedding." From his pants pocket, he produced a black box. Lucifer watched Father as if he was pulling out a gun.

Inside the box was a necklace. It was little gold chains attached to a small heart. It was a copper color with a tiny diamond in the center. I was grinning as Evan gave Lucifer the box so he could hold each end of the necklace. I turned around so he could put the necklace on. Father's fingers touched my neck before pulling my hair out of the chain.

I gave him a huge hug. His grip hurt a little, but I didn't mind. After he released me, Lucifer thanked him and shook his hand.

Father's face lit up, and then it dawned on me I was marrying a guy older than my father. I was going to be sick. My hand gripped my stomach, and then my mouth. In a rush I ran from the room and down the hall. I was in my private bathroom, practically heaving my guts out.

CHAPTER 25

Annilia found me in the bathroom. She helped clean me and take me to the bed. After feeling my forehead, she declared me healthy. Deidra came in, holding a black bag. She dropped it next to where I was laying. I heard the zipper, and she started pulling things out.

My eyes were closed, but I could tell the next person to enter was Beatrice. She also had a bag, but she didn't open it. Even though my stomach hadn't settled, and I was ready to collapse, I was forced to my feet. They all pounced on me, claiming a different part of me as if I wasn't here. Deidra had me changed into new clothing. Annilia was working on painting, not only my nails, but my face. Beatrice was working on hair and earrings.

They finished with me and went to taking care of themselves. I looked in the bathroom mirror. I had a black skirt to my knees. The shirt I had on hung by one shoulder and dipped dangerously low on the other. My face was caked with makeup, and my nails were red. I took a daring look down my freshly waxed legs. I had on stilettos. Did someone forget I was only sixteen?

When I turned to see my sisters, they had on very similar outfits, except they were all wearing blue. They took me from the room and downstairs. For the first time, I was taken from the castle. A limo was waiting outside for us. Once we were inside, they were passing around a bottle of champagne with the music blasting. Deidra was only eighteen and already following in their footsteps. They were in their twenties and had no one.

"A toast to our baby sister, who will be marrying the king of all demons!" Annilia was shouting over the music with her glass high.

Everyone followed the motion until Beatrice spoke up. "Valencia, we never knew you as well as we should, but we all get to live as sisters, so this night belongs to you."

Everyone drank again, and then Deidra began to stand. The roof opened up and she reached out. "My baby sister is marrying the devil!" Her voice echoed down the road. Horns honked, and everyone started laughing. She sat quickly and finished her glass. The limo went smoothly enough for her to successfully pour a second. "Imagine, we all get to live in a castle. Hey, are you going to be a queen with a crown? I want a tiara with the title of princess." Our laughter filled in the gaps of the music.

The limo stopped. We were at a club. It was easily spotted, because the building vibrated from the music. One by one, we left the limo. It was amazing that I didn't fly away, but I followed them into the building. Annilia led the way and whispered to the bouncer. As big as his muscles were, he started to relax when she spoke. He was laughing and nodding as he lifted the velvet rope. I looked at his green eyes. They were distant.

Once inside, she ran directly to the bartender. Beatrice took me to the back of the room and sat us in the booth. Deidra had disappeared, but she wasn't far. I stopped to take in everything around me. Lights flashed with the beat, and the dancers swayed to it.

"Valencia, are you okay?" I looked at Beatrice.

"I would rather be back on Earth with Mark. You guys do know I'm sixteen, right?"

She laughed but leaned in close. "Bachelorette party, we have a lot planned and we don't care how old you are." I shook my head, but looked up to the girls joining us. Each of them held two drinks. I was given the pink one with cherries. It was gone in just minutes.

"Baby sis, we have a gift for you." Annilia stood and walked away again. Deidra smirked and took my hand. We all went to a separate room. The lights were dim and didn't flash, but we still had the music. Chairs were scattered around. Beatrice sat me in the second one and attacked me with a veil.

The door opened, and I was quickly given another drink. Annilia walked in and motioned to someone behind her. A perfectly sculpted boy walked in. My cheeks were a blinding red, and I looked away. I knew what they had planned. Wasn't it already enough I was being forced into marriage?

The boy with dark, blond hair came closer. He flipped the veil back, and I had to look. His skin was sun-kissed, and his wings were dazzling. With confidence, I stood and pushed my way out the door. I was quick with my exit. When I made it out, I climbed in the limo. I made sure every door was locked.

The girls were storming from the door to the limo. I was yanking the veil off. The driver unlocked the doors so they were able to pounce on me, each yelling about me ditching them. They were lucky I wasn't angry—it would have gone worse. Ten minutes passed before I picked up the bottle that was half-empty. In seconds, I had chugged it dry. They all stopped to stare.

"Can we all just go home? It's a big day tomorrow." They were upset with me, but they agreed.

CHAPTER 26

I was finally lying on my bed. Mark came in to check on me. The nightgown was a new color, but still lovely. He sat next to me as I talked of the night. I stretched my wings out, and he actually started to pet them. My smile enhanced as I looked up at him. His fingers slid up to my shoulders.

"I want you relaxed, not upset."

I let my eyes close and my wings tuck in. "Thank you so much Mark." The door opened, but he didn't stop. What we were doing was so innocent that, no matter who walked in, we would all just be fine.

Lucifer strolled closer as I opened my eyes. He sat behind Mark and just watched us. Mark's fingers kept moving as if he didn't care what would happen to him. Everything was silent, until Lucifer began talking.

"How did the party go?" I started laughing and shook my head.

"They forget I was only sixteen and went wild. Even took me to some club to watch a guy strip." They all chuckled, warming my heart. Mark's fingers lifted, and rougher ones took their place. Mark said good night and walked away. I was left with Lucifer.

"Did you enjoy the club?"

I tilted my head so I could see him better. "No, I left when the guy showed up. Why are you here? Isn't it bad luck to see the bride before the wedding?" He gave a little shrug and removed his hands. I sat up and let my wings fall so I could shake out the feathers.

"Wanted to spend time with you and tell you more of what will happen tomorrow." My hand lifted to gesture him to continue speaking. I knew very well what would happen tomorrow. I was being sold to the devil. My very soul would belong to him. For what, though? So I could live in the castle? Or was it so I could live with my family again?

"Your sisters will come in here early with Alias and help you get ready. There's not an actual bouquet of flowers; it's more of a skull with flowers popping from its eyes and mouth and you'll be holding the neck. The ceremony will be outside. Each of your siblings will be playing an important role, along with your father. As for your friend, there wasn't much room for him, but he gets a front-row seat, where the remainder of your family will be."

I just nodded. There wasn't enough I could do to change anything about the wedding. I couldn't change grooms, and I couldn't get a new bride to step in for me. "I better get to sleep then. Good night Lucifer." He began to stand but turned to face me. I just watched as he extended his hand. Obediently I took it.

Carefully, he tugged until I was standing in front of him. "May I kiss you good night, Valencia?" My pupils grew at the question. It took every ounce of my strength not to go throw up again. Instead, I just gave a small nod so my mouth wouldn't open, giving it the chance to say no. His hand released mine to hold half of my face. It pulled me closer, and his eyes remained looking at me. His lips met mine and started moving them. I stayed still, but his eyes shut.

When he realized I wouldn't react, he detached himself and left. My feet wouldn't move. I had to clutch my head to keep it from exploding. Thoughts were being shot off and bouncing off each wall of my skull. It was amazing that I was standing.

After my head settled down I rushed to the bathroom. I heaved everything in my stomach. I was hoping it was from the alcohol, but I knew it was from the kiss. It was awhile before I had stopped. I washed myself off as best I could before going to bed.

For an hour, I rolled back and forth. My head was cluttered with horrible thoughts. Every solution either involved killing or running away. Only problem was, that in order for me to run away, someone was going to have to die. Over and over I thought of killing Father. He had caused all of this. He should be the one to pay. With him gone, everyone would be able to survive and have the best lives. Father would finally be punished for all the wrong he had caused.

CHAPTER 27

I awoke to giddy faces. Each had a squeal of happiness when my eyes fluttered open. As predicted, I was met by my sisters and Alias. There was no arguing. I sat up, and they began the torture. One by one, they worked. My nails were redecorated so that they had French tips. Even my toenails got a fresh coat of paint. Before anything else happened, Alias brought out the dress. I was forced to shut my eyes so I would be surprised.

It was white, went past my feet, and flowed out back so it would drag but wouldn't need to be held. It was a complete white all the way to my chest. The sleeves were mesh, with a little pattern of white fabric. Down the side of the dress were white flowers; they were real. Alias's other hand held shoes. They were sandals with one big, pointed heel and laces going up my leg.

Carefully they did my makeup. Yet again I felt like a raccoon, with all the black they used. My lips became a bright red that shined, even without direct light. Each cheek was doused in blush, as if they needed to be any redder.

I was practically begging for the dress to come on when they pulled out more beauty utensils. As much of a girl as I was, I could never do the whole makeup thing. Audrey had taught me that beautiful girls never needed to hide their faces under a pool of harmful products. Of course, she never objected the clear lip gloss, because all it did was make your lips sparkle in the light—not to mention the taste of some of them.

They helped me into the dress and zipped up the back. I was sat down again so they could mess up my hair. If I had any say, it would have remained down. It was already going to be covered by the veil. Every girl took to a new job either curling, brushing, pinning, or spraying. When they had made a perfect clump on my head, they hosed it down with hair spray. The rest came out into little curls that looked like a head of spaghetti. A mound of spray went on before they brushed it out. My head hurt, but they placed the veil on again. It was the same one from last night. They kept it folded back for now.

Annilia stepped outside the room. All the girls sat down for now. Most of their work was done. They all talked and giggled. I remained silent as my anxiety rose. Within ten minutes, she returned. In one hand, she held the "bouquet," and in the other was the garter. It was black, with a bright red bow. My head never shook faster. They held my arms so I couldn't fight. The skull was set down, with the black roses coming out.

She extended my leg, and the garter went on. Before I could snap back to take it off, she slid the shoe onto the right foot. It was tied on tightly so I wouldn't have time to take it off. My frustration rose as they put on the next shoe. I was left to sit there as everyone but Alias went across the hall. They knew better than to leave me alone.

A half-hour faded before they came strolling back in. Each held a small red rose. Their dresses were black and strapless. They went to their knees, with strips of red starting at the bottom and running upward to a point right at their belt, below their breasts. Each had on black flats and makeup. They had all straightened their hair.

A knock took my gaze. My eyes were raptors as I stared down the door. It opened slowly, and Father stepped in. A hand felt along my neck; I was still wearing the necklace. He smiled and came closer. Leaning to me, his arms held me close. One of the girls swatted him away, yelling that he'd wreck their masterpiece. With a laugh, he moved from me and looked at each of my sisters.

"I knew this day would come. You're a woman now, Valencia. I've never been this proud of you before. It's time to make history. Go join your brothers. I get to take the bride down." Everyone scattered from the room. I was left alone with the monster. His smile dropped as the door shut. Even Alias had left me alone. "I know you spent the day with Mark yesterday. As your father, I know it wasn't the innocent get-together. Your ring was taken off. That will never happen ever again." My head tilted for a nod and swiveled to see the balcony. If I wasn't in heels I would have made it out before Father could react. I was trapped.

He went to fetch the skull. My heart raced, knowing this was it. I would never be free again. Gently, it was set in my hands, and he began to walk me out of the room. We went out the front doors again, where I was greeted by Annilia. She signaled to a shadow ahead of us who went sprinting. We walked until I saw the edge of a crowd. They were all seated. Father pulled me back a couple of feet so I wouldn't be seen yet. I knew the wedding was held at the garden from the angle where I was.

Chapter 28

Annilia ran to the crowd. It took only minutes until the music started up. A slow beat took place, but it wasn't the famous tune I would have to walk to. Father watched as, one by one, his children walked down the aisle. Augustus walked Annilia, and he looked into the crowd. His gaze met his wife and kids. Cornelius and Beatrice walked right after them. She was crying from happiness, I hoped. Deidra and Ezekiel strolled down and split at the end. The boys went to right, next to Lucifer. Each girl stood on the left, just waiting.

The music changed, and Father walked to me. I took his extended arm. He quickly flipped the veil over and started to walk me. His nice suit bent just enough so I could hold tight as we went down the aisle. I looked carefully, but recognized no one. The front row had Mark and Virnant. With a closer look, I saw Mother. Her blond hair was dyed white, and she stood with a smile. She didn't have a boy with her this time.

I dared a look ahead of me. There stood Lucifer in a red suit with a black shirt and a flaming tie. The priest behind him was a skeleton in black robes. I bit my lip to keep from laughing. We came closer to the group, and my pounding heart ceased. Our feet stopped a foot away. Father pulled me into a hug and kissed my cheek. He tapped me forward, and Lucifer held out his hand. Father grabbed his forearm, and they shook. I was pulled up next to Lucifer as Father walked away. He sat next to Mark. On the other side of Mark was Virnant. There would be no trouble from Mark this way.

I looked at Lucifer. He gave a wide smile and pulled my veil back. Each pupil grew in wonder at him. Annilia took the skull from me and placed her flower in one of the eyes. Lucifer took my hands. His were much bigger than mine. A minute passed, and we turned to look at the skeleton.

"We are gathered here today to join these two in marriage." I snuck a peek at Lucifer. He was completely focused on the priest. "Today, you will witness history as Lucifer and Valencia are joined in holy matrimony. Forever they will be one.

"Man was created first. His bones had been extracted and doubled into a woman. For every man, there is his perfect woman. His heart was split in two at birth and placed into his other half. There is a soul-mate for everyone. Standing before us is the perfect match." He stopped and looked between us.

"We will now share the rings, since no vows have been written. Before we do so, I would like to ask for anyone who objects to speak now or forever hold their peace."

My eyes looked at Mark. He had tears in his. Father was whispering to him. With a closer look, I saw a gun stuck into Mark's side. I wouldn't be saved. Minutes passed before the skeleton spoke again. "Let the best man and maid of honor bring forth the rings." I turned to Annilia and reclaimed my hand. She gave me a ring. My head turned to see the skeleton. It was aged badly. He looked at Lucifer first. It was typical to turn to the man first—women were nothing here, just trophies.

"Do you take this woman to be your wife? To love in sickness and in health? For better or worse? For richer or poor? Will you love her always?"

Lucifer looked at me and smiled. "I do." His smile grew and I looked even more at the skeleton. The top had a crack running through. It was polished clean for the wedding.

"Do you take this man to be your husband? To love in sickness and in health? For better or worse? For richer or poor? Will you love him always?" I looked into the crowd. Father was smiling, but he had pushed the barrel in deeper. A pang shot through my heart, and then nails dug deep into my hand. I had been quiet too long.

"I do." Tears dripped down my face.

We placed the rings on and looked at the priest. "By the power vested in me I claim you husband and wife. You may kiss the bride." Lucifer came close and pulled me into him hard. He kissed me yet again, and I still didn't respond. His eyes shut, and mine wouldn't. In a flash, his wings came out and wrapped around us so we couldn't be seen. Many laughed, but he pulled away.

"You belong to me now. As my wife, you will show, or, one by one, I will take away your siblings and Mark." I nodded, and his wings pulled away. Everyone stood and clapped as he rushed me down the aisle. At the end, I noticed there were several cameramen snapping pictures. One had been videotaping the whole thing.

Lucifer turned to watch as people began to leave. I held his arm tighter, and he took me inside. The big doors remained open, and we stood next to them. We would be greeting the guests, not as two people, but as husband and wife. During that time I was introduced to dozens of strangers. Mark entered last. He shook hands with Lucifer and gave me a hug. It was short and hurt us both.

Chapter 29

Everyone was taken to the ballroom. It had been set up with tables everywhere along the edges. The head table wasn't round like the others—it was a long rectangle facing the band. A large flower was set in the center. My bouquet was set in the center of it so that its petals still showed. Every table had white cloth.

Lucifer and I had special throne-type seats. Everyone else had cushioned small chairs. There was champagne in front of everyone. To my right were all my sisters. On Lucifer's left were all my brothers. The table closest to us held all the people I knew, who weren't enough to fill it.

"Once everyone is settled, we will dance. I want a real kiss this time." Lucifer's head was pressed tightly to mine so no one could hear him. With a nod, he pulled me to my feet.

Alias walked to the center of the room and clicked her heels so everyone would look. She was actually dressed in a long skirt and a beautiful blouse. She had changed from when I had seen her. "Now I would like to introduce the new couple as they start life together with their first dance." Everyone clapped as he pulled me to where she had once stood. Cameras flashed as the music went on. It was a slow song. We came together, and my left arm lifted and bent so the hand touched his shoulder blade. My right hand grasped his off to the side. We swirled around. He wore a real smile, and mine was forced.

Minutes passed before he leaned in to kiss me again. This time I kissed back and dropped his hand so I could grasp his hair. Everyone clapped until we went back to dancing. A quick glance revealed that Mark was leaving. Father rushed over instantly and took me from Lucifer. I had my first father-daughter dance in front of strangers.

The music ended, and I practically ran to my table. Lucifer took my hand and held it there.

I scanned the room and watched people come in, carrying trays of food. Salad was placed in front of everyone. It was the brightest green, and far from wilted. Bright-red tomatoes sat next to round olives. Carrot slivers clung to onion chunks. Dressing was drizzled thickly so that not a piece would be dry. My best guess was that it was Italian.

Before I could grab my fork Annilia stood. I went red and she lifted her glass banging her knife off it. Every sound was silenced and every head turned to see us. Augustus stood as well holding his glass. Everyone held up theirs.

"A toast, to my baby sister Valencia. She has found the perfect man, and I hope they never stop the honeymoon phase. I remember when she had those tiny wings, and we were trying to teach her to fly. If she had Lucifer on the other side, those wings would have worked the first time. I love you and I always will." Everyone took a sip and laughed a little.

"My sister and Lucifer—I never saw this day coming," Augustus broke in to fill the silence. "Aren't they something? She's so young and spry, and he's been ruling Hell since its creation! Only they could love each other. May their marriage be a happy one. Oh, and I want some kids to start calling me uncle." Everyone laughed for minutes straight before drinking their champagne.

It was Father who stood next. Every eye looked at him, and my heart accelerated. "You are my only baby girl and the one who has made me proud. Valencia, I wish only for you to be happy and in the right hands. I trust those hands that are attached to him. I will love you with all my heart, and I will never stop loving you. So enjoy every moment. Even those little fights will be memories you wish to relive over again." Again, everyone drank, and many needed refills. Servants rushed around with bottles to meet those demands. We were told to dig in, but the door opened, and heels clopped in, making us all turn. My eyes watered, and I sprung to my feet when I saw the face. Lucifer gripped my wrist tightly to keep me from running.

CHAPTER 30

Audrey walked in with pure white wings glowing in the light. Her eyes smiled when she caught mine. She was in an elegant purple dress to her knees that had a slit on one side. She was gorgeous with her brown, flowing hair. Her hand was raised, holding a glass. As she sauntered in farther, her black heels clicked.

"I have one thing to say to Valencia. She has been a daughter to me since she came into my life—every cut I cleaned and every tear I wiped. She is my whole heart and will forever live in it. I love you, Valencia, I always will, and nothing will ever stop me. No matter what you decide, I will back you up completely. As for you, Lucifer, I am trusting you with the one thing that means the world to me—now, release her so I can hold my angel." A few gasped, and others were too speechless to dare utter a word. I was given my arm back, and I rushed to Audrey. I never held anything tighter. She laughed, holding me just as tightly.

"Where have you been?" I nearly screamed out the words, but a tear made me choke on them.

She wiped it away and kissed my cheek.

"They had me tied up with work, so I couldn't come visit you. We'll talk later I promise." I hugged her again and returned to my husband. His eyes were not happy, but he held a smile. I was practically beaming in joy. Audrey went and sat next to Father. Mark slipped in just in time to see she had taken his seat. He went and sat next to her and nearly yelped when he was told who she was.

It took so much strength to take my eyes away. Once I managed, I ate my salad. Lucifer kept peeking at me as he ate. My heart finally slowed, and I felt trapped again. This is what I would have to live with every day I breathed. Not only was Father pulling strings to keep me his puppet, but Lucifer could just blink and someone would pounce and kill those dearest to me. I no longer belonged to me—I was merely a toy for them.

"We can dance again before the main meal." His words were soft, but it wasn't a question I couldn't object; it was an order. I nodded, and he signaled to someone in the background. The music began again, and I finished off the salad. Many people stood and migrated to the dance floor. Lucifer basically dragged me there.

This time, when we danced, he was more human, as if he knew it'd make me feel better. My hands were around his neck, and his held my waist. He led us in circles and steps around the room. This time, my smile wasn't forced. Mark came over and cut in, so I practically glowed. I let my head rest on his shoulder, and we moved slowly.

"Audrey is so nice. How can she be the sister of your father?"

I shrugged my shoulders. "They're twins; she's the youngest. It's like yin and yang. He took the dark side, and she's on the side of the light."

His eyes opened a little more. We normally never admitted that the two were twins. They were so opposite, but looked so similar. "Well I think the meal is coming. Can you and her meet me later tonight so we can be introduced properly?"

I grinned and agreed before going back to the head table. Lucifer was frowning, but didn't say a word. I would have to learn to keep myself perfect in public so it wouldn't embarrass him. Plates came spinning out. I looked down at the one sitting in front of me.

A bright-red lobster was mounted over a huge steak. It was surrounded by vegetables and fries. Everything was steaming, so it was all freshly made. No one spoke, but everyone dug in at the same time. I laughed to myself as I tried cracking the lobsters. Lucifer wanted to help me, but I wouldn't let him. I wasn't a child anymore, according to father.

He finished first and drank some more before he ordered a wine instead. I was given one too as I polished off the fries. The whole dinner had been lovely, with only the best tastes. My glass emptied quickly, and I looked around the room. Many stood to dance again. This time it was Ezekiel who had asked me to dance.

Again, I had my arms bent at angles to dance with him. He congratulated me, but I didn't feel like a winner. In my head I was a failure for caving into their demands. It was Cornelius who asked me next. He was more silent, but smiled more.

"I heard you were engaged." He went pale white and almost stopped moving. "Beatrice told me, is she here? I would just love to meet her."

His color slowly came back, and he shook his head. "She wouldn't come. She's an angel just like you and Audrey." I made a sad face but we continued to dance.

Augustus didn't get his turn, because it was time for cake. They rolled out a huge mountain of black frosting. A red dragon was created to wrap around it. It had fire blowing at a tower on top that held a princess. She had my face. In front of her was Lucifer, holding out a shield to block the fire. He had thrown his sword to hit the dragon; it was in midair. I was baffled, but all the guests were in awe. The cameras flashed and took position to watch the ceremonial sharing of the cake.

Lucifer cut a tiny slice from the bottom. Inside was a red, moist hunk surrounded by frosting. He smiled and lifted it to me. Instantly, I opened my mouth and ate it. Every taste bud burst in excitement. I never tasted anything so rich. Carefully I cut him a piece. He ate it and then held my hand. Cameras flashed, and he swallowed. As if he had a script, he leaned in for a kiss. Being his wife, I kissed back. When everyone stopped clapping, we passed out the cake, and I was able to sit once more.

I ate my slice and drank from my refilled glass. Annilia kept poking my leg with her foot as she ate. Each time I looked at her, she wiggled her eyes brown, indicating the worst. Once my hand fell and I felt my leg through my dress. She was pointing out I still had the garter on. The beating in my chest halted, and I looked up at Lucifer. He grinned and winked, knowing why my smile had dropped.

This time I ate slowly. Even after it had vanished, I drank the speed of a snail. I had nothing left to procrastinate with, so I took Annilia's arm and made her dance with me. It was Father who had caught on to my little game. He brushed my sister aside so he could join me.

"We fixed your bouquet so it was throwable. After this dance, we will line up all the girls, and you can throw." My head shook, but his face went cold and still. He didn't blink. I nodded and sighed. He was my master, but by tonight, he would be giving the keys to someone worse. The song ended, and he took my hand. Roughly, he pulled me to where the skull was; the flowers had been removed and tied together. He handed it to me before tapping a glass. Everyone turned and saw what I held. One by one, all the single girls went to stand on the dance floor. Father turned me so my back was to the crowd.

I took a deep breath and held the flowers in both hands. I heaved them over my head and turned to see who would catch it. My eyes lit up when I saw a little girl holding the flowers. She was beaming as she rushed to her mother. It was Augustus's little girl. He smiled and winked at me. My heart melted slightly, knowing how he felt. She would be the next to marry. I only hoped her parents let her wed anyone she wanted.

Lucifer came up to me and took my hand. I was trembling as he led me to the center of the room. Father pulled a chair so I could sit in it. As I did, my ribs nearly broke from the way my heart was beating against them. It couldn't escape, so it started moving up. I had to bite my lips to keep from puking.

Lucifer squatted in front of me. He smirked and took my foot. Pulling it out from under me, his other hand extended up. Each finger went slow, so it would run over the skin smoothly. He touched the small piece fabric and looked up at me. He started to tug, but when he saw my relief, he stopped. Again his fingers went up. They grazed my panties, and my other leg tapped him. He chuckled, but went back to the garter and removed it. Standing up, he looked to see if everyone had lined up. With that, he turned and tossed it.

My jaw dropped when I saw Mark holding it. He only smiled and placed it in his pocket as he went back to his table. Lucifer was mad, and I could tell by the way he lifted me up to take me back to our table. He didn't budge, but continued to drink. Wanting to get away, I ran to Audrey, and she danced with me. She understood my pain and just held me as we swayed.

"Take me home." Tears danced in my eyes as I looked at her. She looked away.

"This is your home, but I get to live here with you in your old room. We can have sleepovers, and it will be like the old days." Even she couldn't save me. I had been lost forever with only one way out—I would have to die.

CHAPTER 31

Everyone danced for a few hours before Lucifer took me to sit. Containers of presents were rolled out, and it was time to open them. Our chairs were moved so we could have easy access. There were several bins. Only one held all of my family's. I let Lucifer open all the presents from his friends. He mainly was given money since there wasn't much he needed. One gave us a getaway to an island on Earth. Lucifer wasn't happy, but he thanked him anyway.

Among his presents looked to be some of the oddest things. There were skeletal ornaments and paintings that were priceless. Nothing here was what would be given to the average couple. There weren't appliances or anything of that measure.

The last bin was rolled up to me. I looked at my family. Mother and Father were holding hands. It was either an act or a miracle. With a brighter smile, I took out the first present. It belonged to Audrey. There was no card, only a square box. Inside was her necklace. It wasn't just any necklace, but the one she would wear every day. It was a heart-shaped ruby with diamonds around it. To me, it always symbolized the heart of an angel. I thanked her a million times as I put the silver chain on.

Carefully I pulled out another box, but this one was bigger. Inside was a woven old blanket. I had seen it many times before when I was little—it had always sat on my parent's bed. It had come from only father. He chuckled and spoke up, "It's a baby-making blanket. I want grandchildren before I get too old." I laughed nervously and put it back inside. If only he knew he was already a grandfather.

Shaking my head, I turned to the next present. Lucifer handed me two cards. Mother had given me a hundred dollars, and Cornelius gave me ten times that amount. After thanking them, I lifted up a square box. It was bigger than the last one. Inside was a tiara with many colored gems. Beatrice had handcrafted it for me. Instantly, I placed it on. She beamed in joy and hugged me.

The next box came from Annilia. I was practically terrified of opening it. She was smirking as I popped the lid open. I nearly regurgitated all my food from what I saw. Inside was a mesh nightgown, obliviously for tonight. Lucifer smiled, and he lifted it so we could see it better. It was short, with tiny straps. A bunny symbol rested in a corner. Against my will, I thanked her, but put it aside next to Father's.

I took out a painting next. On it was the whole family, including Mother holding Father and Audrey on the side. The only new member was Lucifer, and he was holding me. I looked in the corner. Deidra had painted it, and it was perfect—minus the one flaw of having Lucifer in it. With a big smile, I thanked her.

Next, I lifted up an old wooden chest. It was small and had my name carved into it . . . next to Lucifer's. Opening it, I found a tea set inside. A piece of paper rested in one of the cups. Everything was white and gold. I opened the letter and read out loud. "Dear Valencia, I got this for you when I was on Earth. It reminded me of the times I would visit Audrey when I was little. She had a similar one at her house. So I got this one for you so you would feel at home. Love, Augustus." I smiled and thanked him. This meant a lot to me.

Again I found a box. It looked just like the one that had the nightgown. This time, it opened to a dress. It was beautiful, purple silk that had small flowing shoulders and came to my feet. It had a black studded belt right were the V-neck ended. On the inside of the box, it read "Ezekiel" and had the name of an Earth store on it—Macy's. I couldn't do anything but thank him.

The last box had Mark's name on it. I tore open the package, and it was another box; this one was rectangular. It was painted with an angel in the woods. She had a few black streaks on her wings. The face was mine, and all I could do was smile. My finger grazed the back, and I felt a key. With excitement coursing my veins, I twisted it open. A lovely melody filled the room as I looked down to see a picture. It was him standing in front the cabin right where the tent had been.

My happiness got the best of me, and I sprung up to hug him. Lucifer's hand missed my arm before it swung around Mark's neck. I went to sit again, and Lucifer frowned. We thanked everyone yet again as someone came in, putting all the presents in the containers. I whispered to one of the people to put the music box in my room, where Audrey would be staying. She would keep it safe. I keyed in my aunt, who hugged me as an answer.

I went to get a drink again when Lucifer pulled me away to go dance. His strength made me stay with him for a half-hour. I watched as people had more cake and partied on. An hour passed, and several started to go. I had to watch Augustus say good-bye to his little family. I would make it a priority to have them living here soon.

When it was down to one final table of guests, I was allowed to go drink. A glass of wine vanished, and Mark took its place. He led me to the dance floor, where we swayed to the soft beat.

"Your present was the best. How'd you think of it?"

He blushed a little, but his lips only curled more. "I knew you would want something to remember me by. A picture is worth a thousand words." I hugged a little tighter, and we swayed with the beat. Time was slow, until Father pulled me away. We were split up again, and I was forced to go dance with Lucifer for the remainder of the guests. When they vanished, so did I.

CHAPTER 32

With Audrey by my side, we escaped to the library. We hid way in the back, safe behind the books. She smiled even more, and I ruffled out my wings. I took off the veil and undid my heels. She helped as best she could.

"Where have you been?" I was finally relaxed up against the wall. She was sitting in front of me so I could see her.

"They had me down in the dungeon since the trials. Everyone thought I would bust you out. They took my bow and followed you. They had set everything up to make it look like I was hiding on Earth so they could tell you I was dead. You will never believe how brilliant they can be. Now tell me about Mark."

I half-smiled at her. She at least was safe. "I met him on Earth. He was underneath a tree, and I helped save him. My powers were fading, so I healed him as best I could. We had a date the next night. Then I stayed over. He caught me getting ready to fly until I wanted sleep. He took me inside and held me until I fell asleep. The next day I showed him my wings, and I told him the story that night. We fell in love and fell asleep in the woods. That morning, we had gone to breakfast. Father had claimed me missing on TV. Annilia had posed as a friend staying with them. I was locked up until father came. Mark fought to stay with me, and here he is in this castle with us." She smiled and stood. I was left sitting there, as she claimed to be back soon.

Patiently I waited for her return. The whole time, I was thinking of any way to avoid tonight. Every fiber of my being was against just kissing Lucifer—there was no way I could have or even make a child with him. I was sick even thinking about it, and there was no way I could handle being sick again tonight. If it kept me safe, I wouldn't mind, but even vomit wouldn't keep him away.

Audrey returned, not only with a platter of food, but with Mark. We all stayed in the back, munching on sandwiches and crackers with cheese. They talked to each other more so she could get a feel for who he was. The platter had emptied, but no one dared to go get more, or even drinks. We could hear people shouting my name repeatedly.

"Valencia, if you don't go, someone will die." My head dropped, but I stood. Hugging each one of them, I left. I walked out of the library and to the stairs. It was there that I had found Lucifer. He looked relieved when he had finally spotted me. Rushing down, he gave me a hug.

"I have been worried sick." He didn't bother asking where I was or who I was with; he just took my hand and pulled me up the stairs.

Down the hall we went. When the doors to his room opened, I was amazed. On one side were two large dressers with plenty of space on top. Only one had a mirror. The bed was huge and had an ocean of pillows on top. It was mahogany wood, with skulls carved in. There was a red net draped down. Beyond the bed was, not only a private Jacuzzi, but an even larger balcony. It stretched farther out, and vines wrapped around it.

I glanced into one of the open doors. The bathroom was huge. It had a walk-in shower with three different heads and its own three-person bath. There were two sinks that just hung in space. But behind the mirror was a cabinet that went very deep into the wall, so it could hold anything. The towels were fluffy and white.

"Welcome to your new room." I turned to look at him. The second I saw his face and the look he wore, I was clutching my stomach again. In a flash, I was hanging over the gold toilet, releasing my dinner. Lucifer came in and held my hair back. When I had started just dry heaving, he tried to help wash everything off. I tried to keep him away, but he insisted on helping me.

"I just want sleep." He laughed softly and pulled me to my feet.

"It's our wedding night, Valencia. Don't you want to remember it?" I sent daggers through him with my eyes. If only they were real.

"No. I want to sleep." His smile dropped, and I yanked away from him. I looked at the dresser and picked the mirrored one. Sure enough, it had woman's clothing. I dug through several drawers before he came behind me. Gently he pulled me to my feet. Annilia's gift wavered in front of me.

"Is this what you're looking for?" I took it in my hands, and he released it. Suddenly I let go and started to stomp on it.

I never saw it coming. All I felt was pain, and, when my eyes opened, I was on the floor. He was above me with a blank stare. "Put it on, Valencia. We're married now. You have to listen to me."

I nodded and sat up. After taking the material to the bathroom, I changed. One look in the mirror had me throwing up again. None of this was me. I was a doll to them.

Lucifer came in and held my hair again. He sighed, seeing how this night was going to go. There would be no agreeing to his terms. This time when I stopped, he sat behind me and put me on his lap. I didn't fight him. He held me and kept his chin on my shoulder so I was tucked into him tightly.

"What will make you be okay with loving me?" My eyes were squeezed together tightly. He was trying to reason with me, but nothing would change my feelings.

"Nothing. Let me be with Mark tonight, and I'll be better tomorrow. Show that you care how I feel, and I'll accept you more." He went still, and I held my breath. Everything was silent. He broke it all with a sigh.

"If I let you, will you stop fighting me every step of the way? Will you be willing to share your everything with me?" This was my chance, and I had no option but to grab the bull by the horns and run off to Mark.

"I will fight less, but you have to remember, I won't be okay with everything. If you go slow and gentle, I promise I will get better that way." He nodded, and I took off at a full sprint. I had no cares as to how I looked. Mark wasn't in his room yet, but I took it as a chance to look around.

I flopped onto his bed and waited for him. My heart raced as he opened the door. The look on his face was enough to prove his love. He came rushing to my side. I took off my rings and let them hit the floor. His arms pulled me into him so hard that I could feel almost every bone in him.

"Why are you here?" He started to pull his tie off.

"Lucifer said I could spend the night with you. Mark, I want you *now*."

His chuckle warmed my heart as I pushed his jacket off. "You sure he's okay with all this?"

My nod started our night. Mark and I made love. Nothing would ever compare in my head. Hours later, we were still under the covers, cuddling and kissing still. The way we panted was adorable to us.

"Valencia, I love you. Promise never to forget me." I kissed him again and promised.

CHAPTER 33

It was hours until we had fallen asleep. I had tucked us safely under my wings so no one would see us. The afternoon sun had risen when I awoke. Mark was already up, smiling at me. He was propped on one elbow, and his other arm was on my hip, keeping me steady so I wouldn't hurt my wings if I rolled.

"Good morning, Marky." I gave him a kiss, and he held me closer. Our lips parted, and I drew in my wings so I could snuggle close. His arm encircled me so I was pressed to him. My ear was against his chest so I could hear his wonderful heart.

"Take my shirt and keep it with you. Whenever you miss me, put it on. It'll be like I'm holding you." I kissed him again and just held him. Someone knocked on the door, and I hid under the covers. He sat up and told the person to come in.

"Have you seen Valencia?" It was Audrey's voice. Quickly, I pulled myself up to smile at her. She laughed, shutting the door. She walked to us and sat on the edge of the bed. I was practically glowing as I watched her.

"I can tell you both had a wonderful night. Mind telling me how you pulled it off?" She directed the question to me. My cheeks reddened, but I told her what had happened. Mark was even a little surprised.

"Might want to get to your room quickly and prove you weren't just playing him." I kissed Mark again and got up. Putting on my rings and nightgown, I went to the door. Mark motioned to the closet, and I went inside. Audrey sighed and stood behind me. She took his shirt, promising to keep it safe in her room. Blowing a kiss to him and giving her a hug, I went across the hall.

Lucifer was still asleep when I snuck in. He must have gone to bed early this morning. With a deep breath, I crawled in next to him and kissed his cheek. His eyes fluttered open, and then he smiled. Without a word, I gave him a kiss. He responded quickly, but pulled away just as fast.

"Valencia, you have proved yourself. I will have someone bring us breakfast, so go shower." I gave him a little peck before flying off. Making sure the bathroom door was shut, I dropped the nightgown. The water went on hot, and I entered. It was wonderful. It was just right. It was paradise in here. Only once did I hear him call and ask if I needed help. I responded with a no, but when I came out in a fluffy bathrobe, I made sure to give him another kiss. A tray had come in, holding every breakfast food known to man. A bowl of fruits was in the center, surrounded by many different eggs and toast. There were even different types of bacon.

I started with the ham-and-cheese omelet and watched as Lucifer had sausages. We hadn't shared words. I was practically starving, and I ate a sample of everything. He watched me more, than ate. I guzzled down several glasses of orange juice while he laughed. I ate another slice of bacon and questioned him.

"Never seen a girl eat so much in one sitting, but go on I'm sure you're hungry."

I bobbed my head and continued eating. "What are we doing today?"

He popped another sausage in his mouth before he answered. I filled my mouth and waited. "I figured we could stay in bed today. If we're alone, we can do as you say and work ourselves slowly into a normal marriage." My head moved to indicate I was okay with it as I ate some more.

"What about the honeymoon?" Curiosity had gotten the best of me.

"Well, I wasn't going to push on it so soon, but we can go to Earth and visit that hotel. We have a room reserved." Something in me jumped. He had listened and cared what I thought. So it wasn't the way I hoped but it was close enough to prove I was something.

He and I finished off the whole tray. It wasn't long after that someone had come up to retrieve it. When the door shut, Lucifer took me in his strong arms. "Just kisses for now. You can stop me when you need to." He was trying his hardest.

I gave him a kiss, and we went from there. Each one got a little longer. It wasn't long before I stopped him. Not allowing him the chance to question this, I asked about his life. He gave me the same story that we had learned when we were little. He rebelled first and fell. I felt like sleeping it bored me that much.

"Can I nap?" He lifted me up, bridal style. Setting me on the bed, he pulled the covers over me. His head came down and gave me a kiss. I rolled over and went to sleep.

CHAPTER 34

I dreamt of Mark. He and Lucifer were fighting. Mark had died, and I wasn't allowed near the body. I cried and begged, but I was dragged back inside the castle. I was locked in the tallest tower. Audrey had been killed outside my window, followed by my siblings and mother. Father was the one who was to look after me, and Lucifer would come play. It was a nightmare.

I jolted up straight and awoke. My heart pounded and my breathing was heavy. I was in a cold sweat, and seeing Lucifer only made me scream. He made calming noises and tried to hold me. Minutes passed before I relaxed and got my bearings. It took awhile until I eased into him and shut my eyes. I apologized, but he wouldn't accept it. I looked at the balcony. The sun was lowering.

"You've been out a few hours. I can order us dinner if you're hungry." I smiled and kissed his cheek.

"All I want is to unwind. Could I get a little bowl of stuffing or soup?" He nodded and got up. I shut my eyes and lay down again. Lucifer came back and joined me.

He just held me. "Would you like to try the Jacuzzi? It should help you relax." He had been so good to me that I just nodded. I sat up and he pulled a swimsuit from the drawer. I stood up and took the material. Once in the bathroom I changed.

I looked in the mirror. It was plain and black, except there was no backing—only the rear was covered. It was decent, so I couldn't complain. I brushed my hair out and exited the room. Food was here. There was both soup and stuffing. I smiled and picked up the soup first. Lucifer told me I could eat at the same time. I shook my head, but drank the soup and ate the noodles. I left the stuffing for when I got out.

After I had gotten in, he turned on the jets and went to change. My head rested back, and my arms floated. I let my eyes slip closed. Even when the door opened, I didn't budge. He sat across from me, and I heard switches flip. His feet tangled with mine, and I started to look. The water was changing colors. I looked to see him sitting there, smiling at me. My eyes wandered. He was the sculpted one. A minute passed before I swam up to him. His laugh filled my head, but he pulled me to him.

"If I had known, this would have worked, I would have never worn a shirt when I saw you."

I giggled and shook my head. "It wouldn't have worked, then. You proved to me that you cared about what I'm feeling just enough so that I could have the night of my life. Plus, as your wife, I'm supposed to appreciate my husband." He didn't reply with words. Instead he gave me a kiss. Gently, he slid me up onto his lap so he could hold me better.

When he broke away he finally spoke. "Valencia, are you comfortable around me?" His question shocked me. It knocked me off guard, so the look I gave him was blank.

"I am now. Before, I was terrified to be alone with you and now I don't mind so much." He just nodded and kissed me again. This time, he leaned me back some so my head could rest on one of the cushions. His lips broke off briefly, but found my neck instead. My heart pounded when I felt teeth. I started to push him back.

He looked up with red eyes. "Angel blood tastes the best." His voice was monotone, and his face was hungry. He didn't say another word; he just took my hands, which were on his shoulders, and placed them by my side. They stayed there as he came back, this time biting. His teeth went through my skin, and I screamed. Minutes passed until he moved away.

I never moved faster than when I went to hide myself in the bathroom. The door locked, and I stared at the mirror. Blood dripped from the teeth marks. I reached for a towel and wet it. Trying my hardest, I managed to clean the wound just enough. My heart slowed, and I sat on the side of the tub. At least ten minutes passed until he knocked.

"Valencia, open this door. I can clean and heal the wound. Let me explain myself." I stood and rested against it. There would be no way I was coming out that easily. "In order to restore you I had to take some of your effects. That's another reason why you still can't heal. I needed that power the most, in case you get hurt. I took your thirst for blood completely. In the next few feedings, I won't crave it as much. I'm sorry I hurt you." He walked away, and the main door closed.

CHAPTER 35

I opened the bathroom door and checked to make sure he was gone. Once I knew he was, I changed into a cotton dress. Looking out the main door, I skipped into Audrey's room. She was on her bed, writing. Her eyes were relieved when she saw me in one piece. Leaving her papers, she came and held me.

"How is he?"

She knew who I meant, and I saw her grin. "He actually hasn't stopped smiling. He was in here a few minutes ago, before I heard you scream. Sorry I didn't come."

I shrugged off her apology. "Can I stay with you for a while?"

She nodded and cleared the bed so we could sit. We sat there for some time, and she talked a little about Mark. She finally asked of Lucifer, and I told her what had happened. By the end, she was holding me and rubbing in between my wings.

She promised everything would be okay, but Lucifer opened the door. He didn't ask if I was ready; he told me it was time to join him. Audrey hugged me, and I walked past him and out the door. He shut it and turned me so my back was against the wall. There were no words—he only lifted his fingers and placed them on my neck. Minutes passed before he healed it.

"I never said I'm sorry before, and you were the first to hear it."

I looked at him, but wouldn't smile. "Let me go where I want tonight, and tomorrow I'll be better than I was today." He sighed and pulled me toward the room. This wasn't a conversation for everyone to see. Once inside, I leaned against the door. He couldn't block it if I was on it.

"If I can feed, you can stay with Mark again, but he goes home tomorrow." Teeth dug in my lips and I could taste blood.

"Deal."

He pounced, pushing me into the door. His teeth gripped my neck again, and they dug in deeper, tearing at the skin. I had to tighten my fists to keep from pushing him away. He finished and started to kiss the wound so it would heal, and not a drop would be wasted. The second his lips parted, I had shoved him back and ran from the room.

Mark was outside his, waiting. Audrey's door was shutting, and I knew why. I ran to him, and he lifted me and spun us in a circle. Once our feet touched the ground, we were flying into his room. I stretched my wings out as I gave him a kiss. He was just happy to see me.

"I've missed you." His voice was barely above a whisper as he pulled me close. The kisses he gave me were hungry and relentless.

"You have to go home tomorrow, so we must make tonight special." He didn't dare question why. Instead, his fingers tore at my dress.

CHAPTER 36

Mark and I could never have been closer by the time we woke up trapped in my wings. I had awakened first and just beamed at him. When I caught his eyes fluttering, I gave him a tiny kiss. Once he saw me he pulled me closer. I pushed him away and set my head on his chest. I was trying to remember not only how he felt, but his heartbeat and his scent. It was indescribable. It was like smelling fresh cookies and made you warm and fuzzy inside.

"I got to go. I'll be back soon, Marky." He gave me a kiss. I got up and put on what was left of the dress. After blowing him another kiss, I started to leave. I looked down the hall to where my room was. Beatrice was sneaking out of it, and she went running. I only shrugged it off and walked across the corridor. Silently I opened the door and made sure it didn't slam behind me. Lucifer was lying in bed, looking asleep.

I crept close and pulled the covers down a little so I could crawl in and surprise him when he awoke. After a moment, I finally settled in, sure I hadn't disturbed him. My eyes were closing, and I was getting ready to sleep. It was unbelievable how exhausted I was. All thoughts were draining rapidly. My brain was fading out.

Lucifer began to stretch, and I tried to ignore it. I couldn't when his arms wrapped around me. He pulled me into him so there was no space. He didn't have a shirt.

"You returned, Beatrice, are you ready for more?"

I shrieked at his dreamy voice. He wasn't asleep once my scream met his eardrums.

His arms flew off, and he rolled off the bed. "You really slept with my sister?"

Lucifer looked down at me. He had that expression every guy wears when he gets caught—they're all thinking of a way to get out of it. "She was more willing than you."

I scoffed and got up. Opening the dresser, I searched for clothing I could fly in. "She wants you more than I do anyways, so go marry her."

His sigh filled the room. He came over and dropped next to me. His hands tried to pull me to him, but I kept yanking away. "Maybe you're the one I want."

Something in me growled, and I prayed it was my stomach. "Don't sell me that crap!" I grasped my mouth just as quickly as I had said it. Things were changing, and I hoped it was because of the wings that I was acting different.

I stood and went into the bathroom. After making sure the door was locked, I got in the shower. Even with the water running over my face, I could feel the tears. I had read enough books to know when a guy was playing you. Whether he was being honest, or not that was a classic line among almost all players.

It was after I had washed at least three times that I shut the water off. I stood in front of the mirror and brushed my hair. After I towel-dried it, I put it into braids. Lucifer hadn't come to the door, but he hadn't left the room. Something in me yearned to know what he was doing out there.

My heart pounded, and I left the bathroom. He was sitting on the edge of the bed staring down the door. At least he put on a shirt. I stayed where I was, not going to be the first one to react. He wasn't the one who had started all the problems, but he had no right to be with my sister. Any other girl would have been fine with me, but not Beatrice.

"He can go home tomorrow, and you can see him later, but you must spend the night here." There it was again. He had to control my life, and the rewards for doing as he said were tempting.

"What are we doing today?" Those dark eyes lit up, and he stood up. My feet shifted back, and he didn't get any closer. Lucifer was easy to read when he was like this. He wanted to come near, but he wasn't going to start a fight.

"You said you'd be better than yesterday. We can try again, but I'd really like to feed."

CHAPTER 37

As hurt as I was, everything was pulling me closer to Lucifer. I had come near enough to touch him without extending my arm fully. He smiled, not only with his lips but with his dark eyes. His hands came up and held my arms. He wasn't hard or aggressive—just gentle.

"Do not fight; do not struggle, Valencia." His voice was calm and steady. My response was a nod. He replied by lifting me. His wings popped out. They were dazzling. The pure, black, silk feathers twinkled from the sunlight. There wasn't a rip or tear in any of them. He used his wings to turn and carry us into the air. I was dazed when he let go. I hit the bed before thinking of opening my own wings. His smile grew as he lowered himself.

Being careful, he landed next to me. His hand connected first, pulling me close. He lowered his head and kissed my cheek. His face dropped lower, and teeth grazed my neck. I bit my lip when his fangs sank in. I tried to relax and remain calm. He didn't take long to finish. After his fill, he made the wound disappear. Lucifer tucked me in under his arm.

"If my actions upset you, I apologize."

I shrugged it off. If I had more space, I would have gotten up and left. "It's my fault all this has happened. If I was born with black wings, Father would have never given me up. I would never have been sent to court. There would be no marriage, and no Mark."

Lucifer took my chin and made me look at him. "Not your fault, it's your father's." Air caught in my throat. Someone else had seen the horrors of Father.

After a minute I started to push him away. He instead pulled me closer and kissed me. Again we built up the kisses until he ordered breakfast. I had an omelet with bacon and cheese inside. We stayed silent until I finished. I left the room, and he didn't push. He already knew where I was going.

Mark was asleep in bed still. I jumped and landed next to him. He started to wake up then he saw me. His smile was huge and growing when I told him he wouldn't go home until tomorrow. He showered me in kisses, as if I had done all this. Even though he didn't like that I couldn't stay here tonight, he was happy we had one more day.

After a while, we sat up and cuddled, our voices soft and sweet as we talked. I couldn't help but stroke his hair. It was so soft today. He only smiled and held me tighter. This was love; I was his other half. It was like my chest held his second heart. We could feel them synchronize—both hearts skipping on the seventy-sixth beat.

"Forever I am yours, Valencia."

I gave him a kiss. He was so sweet. "I want you to remember me always, Marky." I leaned forward and away from him. My wings extended, and I shook them a little. Teeth dug in tight around my lips. My hand lifted and plucked a feather. The pain was instant and sharp. Tears welled in my eyes, and one slipped out. I held the feather in my hand. Mark watched and it began to shiver. I wiped my eyes so I could watch without the blurriness. It had turned white, as if it wasn't affected by the curse. I turned to Mark. "Keep this with you always."

His fingers took the feather and wrapped around me. He gave me more kisses, and I stood. I watched his eyes darken. Neither of us wanted this. Blowing him another kiss, I left. Lucifer was walking to his room when he spotted me. He held the door open, and I went inside. Once it was shut, he hugged me.

I asked, "Where've you been?" He already knew where I was.

"I had some work to take care of. Plus I need someone to fill my place during my absence tomorrow."

I didn't question him. I only put on the swimsuit and got into the Jacuzzi. Lucifer went to the bathroom while the water began to rush in. My head rested on the cushion. As it filled up, I sunk lower.

The door opened, and he walked out wearing those same black trunks. This time he sat closer to me. I didn't dare move. He lifted my legs and set them over his. A hand remained on my left side. It traveled to the foot and squeezed.

"You can either open your eyes, or I break your foot." With that, they opened. I glared at him but his other hand took hold of the same sole. His fingers dug in as if trying to massage it.

"I came back without you asking. If you ask, I'll be more likely to respond happily." He only nodded and pushed his fingers harder.

"Valencia, I scheduled a dinner with your father later. He wants to see you." My eyes bugged, but I agreed. There would be no way around it. Minutes passed before he switched feet. It was nice, but my stomach growled. His right hand moved and grabbed a towel. He dried his hand then picked up a phone. He didn't ask what I wanted; he just called down to Father. We had an hour to get ready.

Once my feet were nice and soft, I was allowed to go and fix myself up. I picked out an elegant red dress. It went past my knees and had drooping sleeves. I fixed my hair so it was up in a bun, a braid running around it to keep it in place. Lucifer knocked, but I didn't answer. I went to find perfume. The door opened instead. He was holding red heels. He helped me in them before leading me out.

CHAPTER 38

Lucifer had led me to somewhere small with just a table set for four. He held my seat out, and I looked to watch as Father and Mother walked in the door. They sat down after Lucifer had shaken his hand. Only plates and silverware were set up along with empty glasses.

"How is the happy couple doing?" Mother asked in that voice hinting the obvious.

I glanced at Lucifer, and he answered. "We are doing splendid. Are you enjoying your stay?" His voice didn't break as it would if he was lying. The only thing concerning me was when his hand landed above my knee and gave a squeeze. It wouldn't move.

Evan finally spoke and eyed me down. "The room is lovely."

"I hope you don't mind but I ordered for us to have fried shrimp over spaghetti. Oh, and Evan, I would like you to try out my office tomorrow. I will show you the whole space on my own time before we bring her friend home." Father's eyes brightened—not at the food but at the office offer. Mother winked at me. She knew something I didn't. They always were a step ahead of me. It was then that Virnant crossed my mind. Where could he have possibly gone?

"You two better enjoy that honeymoon." There it was.

My eyes widened and looked right up at my husband. He gave a nervous laugh. I wasn't supposed to know. He had mentioned it in case we left today, but he never said we would still go tomorrow. Mother blushed and put a hand to her mouth.

Thankfully the door opened, and everyone was given wine. The waiter was a young boy with bad acne. I grabbed his tie and pulled him lower so I could whisper. As low as I could, I told him to keep them coming. There would be no way I could sit here sober, no matter my age.

I watched the boy leave, and another came in holding our plates. The shrimp was battered and fried. It was golden and tasted perfect. There were six large ones. The spaghetti was thick, and there was a mound of it. Three mouthfuls later, I had finished off my first glass of wine. The first boy was back instantly to refill the glass. I nodded and smiled and ate more. Eyes glanced at me, and Lucifer's hand finally moved.

I had finished off three glasses by the time my meal was gone. Evan talked to Lucifer about arrangements, and Mother watched me. She would never be my mom, only a surrogate. If she was a real mom, I wouldn't be here. The doors opened, and dessert came. My glass filled again, and a piece of three-layered chocolate cake sat in front of me.

My plate and glass emptied before the others. My glass was filled again, but I didn't touch it this time. I waited in silence, but smiled. If Father wasn't here I would have run for Mark by now. Lucifer's hand came back to my thigh, but higher up this time.

I tried to get it to come off, but, when I saw no use, I downed the glass. "When did you two get back together?" The questioned stunned them. He gripped my leg harder as if I had spoken out of line. My glass was filled, even though my head buzzed.

"Around the time of the wedding. It made us remember when everything was perfect, and we were getting married," Mother replied, seeing how Father was already displeased. He frowned at me, and I couldn't help but laugh.

"I think it's time for us to depart. Be at my office tomorrow, Evan. I will be waiting." His voice was stern as he eyed my father. Lucifer grasped my shoulders and lifted me as he stood. He dragged me from the room, my feet tripping over each other.

I stifled my giggles until we had gotten to the stairs. They would be my worst nightmare, because I would fall. Instead Lucifer lifted me, bridal style, and flew me to the room. His wings came out, and we were in front of the door in a minute flat. He set me down and opened it. His hand pushed me in, and my heel broke causing me to crash. I laughed so hard I couldn't hear the door slam.

"You embarrassed me tonight, Valencia! How do you plan to make up for it?" I looked up at him.

My face struggled to stay straight. "Not throwing up on you? Maybe if you calm down, we can get somewhere tonight." I felt my cheeks burn, and he brought a hand close to my face. Shyly I took it, and he pulled me into him.

"Where are we going, Valencia?" I bit my cheek. My lips had been bitten too much lately.

"I'm going to bed." Managing to slide the shoes off, I pushed away from Lucifer and just headed there. I collapsed on impact. My wings stretched and shook before tucking in.

Lucifer went to the bathroom. I pulled the covers up and shut my eyes. Even when he came out I knew I couldn't fake being asleep. He crawled in next to me and rolled me over so I had to look at him. His eyes grinned. He didn't bother with words he kissed me. I went limp, hoping this would turn him off.

Chapter 39

Lucifer didn't get much further. I ended up vomiting all over him. He helped me to the bathroom so I had the toilet and he had the sink to wash up with. As I continued he called someone telling them to come clean. My head remained in the toilet as I listened to him talk to the people cleaning.

The door shut, and he joined my side again. He had crackers and ginger ale in his hands. The second I stopped, not only did I thank him, but I ate my small meal. Lucifer lifted me and tucked me into bed. He held me close, and my nose smelt lavender. I relaxed even more.

"I'm sorry, I am a horrible wife."

He shook his head. "We aren't officially married until we make love." I dried heaved and he released me, ready to run to the bathroom again. When nothing more happened I settled down.

"Then we'll never be married."

He chuckled but stroked my hair. "On the honeymoon. Now get some sleep, dear." I obeyed and passed out.

Even though I woke alone, nothing could have made me happier than changing and seeing Mark. Lucifer would know where to find me. I packed everything Mark had in a little bag and waited until he came to. It wasn't long. He gave me a hug and frowned. I had him change into something more comfortable, and then that fatal knock came. We were ready to go—just not ready to part.

Lucifer led us back to where we first came into his castle. The shadows around us looked scary as ever. Mark was close to my side, but wouldn't get closer with Lucifer having an arm around me. We were tossed into a swirling mess, making me want to hurl again. It settled, and we were back in the tomb.

Once above ground, I saw two vehicles waiting for us. There was a black SUV for Mark. Just to rub it in his face, Lucifer had ordered a limo for us. Tearing away from my husband I went to hold my true love. Someone took his bag from him so he could hug back.

"Do you still have it?" My voice barely rose above a whisper, so only he could hear.

"It will never leave my side." I kissed his cheek and watched him go. Not only did the feather leave with him but so did half of my heart. It belonged to him.

Lucifer took me to the limo. It was larger than the one I rode in with my sisters. He gave me a bottle of ginger ale and a handful of crackers. At least he was trying. We drove for what felt like hours; the whole time he was trying to make a pass at me. I could only fight so hard before moving to the other side of the seat. When I finally glanced at him, his arm was bleeding.

"Try again, it's been awhile." It worked this time. As my fingers grazed his forearm, the wound sealed itself shut. I was normal again, and he didn't need blood. He gave me a hug to congratulate me. When the limo stopped, we were on a cliff. "We get to fly there." My excitement couldn't get any higher. I was out of the car and over the edge in under a minute.

CHAPTER 40

My wings ached by the time we descended into Hawaii. Lucifer had a black SUV waiting for us. It drove us to a resort. We were taken into a very big, almost all-glass building. A man in khaki shorts with a gray T-shirt and brown sandals greeted us. He was human, just at a glance. His voice and face were all smiles as he invited us to a wicker couch with puffy, worn cushions.

He sat across from us in a chair and laid down papers on the coffee table in front of us. His name was Jim. Each paper had a different picture. With the room we were given, we could pick a special trip on the island. I let Lucifer choose, and he offered to take the gift and turn it into a couple's spa treatment for tomorrow.

With that, we were given the key to the room and led away. Outside we went and were taken far away. The guide took us down a dock to a medium-sized hut with a straw roof. He opened the door and walked away, assuming we wanted to be alone. I was just glad no one asked if I was too young to be with Lucifer.

I walked in and just smiled. We were greeted by a cozy living room that led to a deck where the water was right below. To the right was a tiny kitchen. Against my will, I looked left and laughed at the open door. Inside was a heart-shaped bed with a bucket of ice and champagne in the middle. Luggage sat near it, waiting to be unpacked. A hand landed on my shoulder pulling me back into a warm body.

"Did you want to toast to our new life together, starting now?" My heart thudded, but I nodded. There was no running or hiding. It was now or death. He probably had the whole area on surveillance to make sure I never left . . . alive.

His hand slid down to take mine. Slowly, Lucifer led me to the room. I sat on the edge of the bed obediently as he went to open the bottle. He handed me the glasses. I heard a pop, and two minutes later, I saw the liquid flow in front of me. He was careful not to spill, even though his eyes begged, hoping it would make me shed a layer. The glass left my hand, and he held it up.

"Valencia, this could become everything you ever wanted: a special room for you in the tallest tower, a daily practice with Virnant, monthly visits to Mark. All I ask is for you to love me and bring to me a son." There was the catch. I was already terrified that, if he knew the truth of what Mark and I had done, there would be no way I could bear a child now.

"To us." I mumbled, and the glasses clanged. My drink vanished, and I reached for a refill. Something in me screamed that this would turn into a habit in the hope of getting sick every night.

"Don't bother, I want you relaxed and remotely into me; so tomorrow after the spa. We can order dinner if you want, then swim." I let the glass fall in the ice bucket and went to use the bathroom. How lovely! It was a sink, toilet, and shower, all cramped in. Guess they didn't think it would be used the most.

I returned to the aroma of lobster and crab legs dancing with melted butter. He had a small table with candles set up in the kitchen. Lucifer held a chair out for me. I sat down and watched him sit across from me. Something in me was hollow. Instead of dwelling, I dug in. He was trying, and it showed. I just hurt too much from leaving Mark.

My plate emptied first, and he told me to go change. The one-piece wasn't in the suitcase. In its place was a fire-red bikini. My face drooped as I slithered into it. I came out to find him already in swim trunks. These ones were maroon. Gently he pulled me out to the deck. A blue hammock rested on one side. Over the rail, we went into the crystal-clear water.

It was bathwater with a salt flavor. Bright fish swam close, but darted away. I spent more time underwater, exploring. Lucifer came and lifted me. He laid me back and spun me in small circles. I eased into him. Eyelids shut so I didn't have to look at his face.

"I love you, why won't you love me?"

I shook my head. "Give me time, and I'll be broken to the point of surrender. Father will make sure of it." He chuckled, but stopped moving and released my legs. My head rested on his shoulder instead.

From out of nowhere, we lifted, and he flew us to the deck. He set me on the hammock and left me there. I curled up and gave a slight push so I could sway.

Lucifer took no time in returning with some drink with cinnamon sticks and powder mixed in. He sat by my side, with him holding me. I drank slowly. The coldness was perfect in this heat. I was half asleep by the time it vanished.

"Valencia, what's wrong? I can make all your pain go away." I shook my head, wanting to get up and leave. He only followed and pestered me.

"This pain will never go. The first time I fall in love, it's banned, and I'm forced to obey Father, who never loved me until he realized I could be used to get him here." My eyes started to flood with tears. I sniffled and blinked, returning my face to a blank stare.

"You love him more than anything?" My head bobbed to say yes. Lucifer sighed. "If you make sure this feeling does not become a problem, then, in a few years, I'll go, and you can have him. Starting now, I want you to act like a wife. No more depression, and no more Mark thoughts. Just smile. Be who you were before you were cursed. If not, I will get someone to wipe your memory." I shivered, but understood what he was saying. With a nod I got up.

Placing the glass in the sink, I went to my room. After entering the small bathroom, I got into the shower. The water was lukewarm, but heavenly. After lathering, rinsing, and repeating, my light bulb went bright. The water turned off, and I wrapped myself in a fluffy white towel. My head poked out into the room, releasing steam. He wasn't there.

I shut the bedroom door next and dug through my suitcase. Inside was that same nightgown Annilia had given me. With a chuckle, I slid it on. He was attempting to promise me the life I wanted, so why couldn't I act like a real wife? I put the towel back and opened the bedroom door. He was just sitting in the living room. Taking a deep breath, I went to him as silently as I could.

Once behind him I bent over so I could wrap my arms around him. His shock was enough to make me smile. I kissed his cheek before dropping my head to look at him. My hair was still wet.

"We don't have to tonight."

I shook my head and smiled. "Who said we were going that far?" This time he laughed and stood. His arms wrapped around me. It wasn't long before he kissed me. It was a simple little one. Surprisingly, it didn't last long.

"Make a wish, Valencia."

I shut my eyes and sighed. "I wish my wings were white again. Then I'd be me, before everything." Lucifer didn't speak he lifted me instead. Into our room we went, and he dropped me on the bed. His eyes moved a little, and he opened his wings and nodded. As if he had said it, I opened mine. I watched him smile and sit next to me. He took his hands to stretch my wings out. Each finger ran over every feather. It felt wonderful, and they vibrated.

I was grinning with each stroke. The tingle stopped, and his hands followed. I pulled my wings in front of me and beamed in joy. My arms wrapped around my husband, and I pelted him with kisses. He chuckled but fell back, holding me close. Everything felt right again. I was Valencia the angel once more. "I love you." My words were soft in his ears and greeted with pleasant responses.

CHAPTER 41

Lucifer and I didn't make love, but fell in love. We awoke in a giddy tangle. His dark wings were protecting us. I couldn't help but kiss him. He laughed, but returned them. This was marriage—waking up to smiles, knowing you were loved. Nothing could shatter how you felt.

"I had them make us breakfast. I ordered last night. It should be here." We got up and walked out the door. He was right. On the table sat omelets with orange juice and bacon. A separate plate sat, stacked high with toast and homefries. It didn't take long to consume everything.

When it was gone, a knock came. It was time to go. We quickly changed into shorts and T-shirts. Again, we were taken to a new dock and led to a building. This one was large, but made just like the one we were staying in, except it had more rooms and an upstairs. A tanned woman with dark hair and eyes greeted us with a big smile that was genuine.

Inside was lovely. It had a front desk surrounded by palm trees. Soothing noises filled the area, which was decorated with chairs. There were several doors, but only one read "Private." We were taken to a small room to change into robes. Along the wall were boxes to keep your stuff in. Thankfully, they had locks. On the robe were two shadows of palm trees over the heart.

We were then taken to a room that was lit with candles. Two beds were set up that had those cushions for your face. They overlooked a see-through floor where fishes swam. The hostess told us just to lie down and that someone would be in soon. The door shut, and I jumped up on the table.

"Don't worry, I made sure one of us was given this job. Don't want humans seeing our wings." Lucifer's voice was low, so it wouldn't be heard. He sat across from me. We were two feet away. I smiled; he thought of everything. In walked two men. They looked familiar. If I had paid attention, I would have recognized them from the wedding. The taller one with lighter eyes came up to me, holding a towel. His soft voice penetrated my train of thought, so he could instruct what I was going to do. He had me turn around and sit on my knees.

Lucifer hadn't made a peep, except the noise of him lying down. I felt the towel brush against my feet. Fingers traced along my neck, slowly pulling the robe off. It was down to my hips when he had me move and grab the towel. The robe dropped, and the towel covered my backside as I lay back down. I smiled and watched the colorful swirls of fish dance in the crystal water below.

Strong hands started to feel along my back for any tense spots. I heard a muffled chuckle when he found that the areas around my wings had knots. He untangled them gently. Again, his hands moved first to my shoulders, and then to my lower back. Lucifer's hand found mine and pulled it so it was in between us. Our fingers laced together.

I nearly jumped when he started to slide the towel up. When I realized he was just moving it so he could reach my legs, my heart stuttered to its normal pattern. My thighs and calves went to jelly by the time he got to my feet. He finished but came up to my arms. He started with the free one, going over every muscle. In the body alone, there are six hundred and forty named muscles, so the arm had plenty for him to tend to. He moved to the other one.

Both of us were done at the same time and given our robes again. We were taken to a new room with porcelain tubs. We were sat in them while water noises drifted around. Lucifer's was next to mine. They filled up my tub after taking my robe. Thankfully I had left panties on so when the mud came it wasn't a big shock. My hair was pulled back, and I was covered to my neck. It was thick and heavy, so I couldn't move easily.

The door opened and someone sat behind me. I looked back to see Arthur. My eyes darted to Lucifer. He was smirking before he spoke. "Valencia, I want you to be my world. No one will stand in my way. Arthur is here to help you forget Mark. When I believe you are ready I promise he will give you those precious memories back."

I started to struggle with the mud to move far away, but Arthur held on. My screams drowned out his words, but soon my head clouded, and I passed out. I was drifting in a sea of darkness. The water splashed over me, pulling me down.

It wasn't long until I awoke, trembling. The mud had been drained, and I was in a hot tub. Lucifer was holding me, stroking my hair. He was tense, and I knew why. My memory wasn't gone, but I had no clue how. All I knew was I had been drowning before I awoke. Water was seeping in my lungs, making them burn.

"Your screams changed my mind. I cannot hurt you by erasing the one thing that means everything to you." His voice was sincere. My heart thudded. I kissed him before swimming away to the other side so I could see him better. As expected, we weren't dressed as much as I would have liked.

"I understand if you are mad and if you don't want to do anything tonight. I have messed up, and I apologize." There it was again. He was proving his affection. The only problem was that I had no clue why he loved me. We had never met until two days before the wedding.

"Let me think it over. Are we doing anything else here?"

His eyes met mine, and something in me shivered. "Not me, but I made you a special appointments tomorrow. I have surprises to make everything up to you." My eyes widened. I could sense this would be a pattern. If he wanted something, he was going to do anything he could to get it. I didn't dare question, because he wouldn't tell me. "Let's get going, I had dinner ordered while you were out." He got out first and retrieved me a robe. We left with him holding a bag of our clothes.

His arm tucked me close. It wasn't long before we walked in on a man leaving from the other door. Steaks were set up on the table again. Vegetables and fries swam around them. It surprised me that it wasn't extremely fancy, like he had been trying to give. We sat in silence. I finished first, so I went to shower.

I came out to find him in bed. He was rolled to the far corner, facing the other way. Something sparked in me. He was upset, thinking he had hurt me. I knew he was trying to be a good husband

and make us last. He had given me so much, knowing I hated being here. It was time to show him everything was tolerable.

I walked around the heart and stood in front of him. I was still snuggled in the warm robe. It was too soft to part with. His eyes opened, and he faintly smiled. His lips opened to speak, "What are you doing, Valencia?" Lucifer just eyed me in suspicion.

"Honey, we had a spa day today. I'm relaxed like you wanted. Lucifer, you proved your love since we arrived. You've asked for little. It's time I show you that I love you." My hairs stood on end, and my teeth nibbled my lips. He started to sit up and pull the covers off. I glanced away, but then stared into those endless eyes. He was starting to stand, trying to make sure I wasn't going to run. Before he was fully upright I dropped the robe. His eyes sparkled. My arms grew goosebumps. His hands ran over them to warm me.

"You're serious." I knew it wasn't a question, so I didn't answer. I kissed him instead. He had earned it by giving me my wings back and letting me keep my memories of Mark.

CHAPTER 42

That morning when I awoke, he was still holding me. My skin was radiating joy, and Lucifer was asleep. I couldn't help but give him a small kiss before getting in the shower. Knowing him he had already ordered food, so I didn't worry about that. It wasn't long before he found me.

I was right; when we both entered the kitchen, there were more omelets. This time we didn't sit apart. He rested me on his lap so we could feed each other. His smile never faltered as he chewed. It warmed my heart just knowing that this could turn into something better.

When he did stop grinning, there was a knock on the door. It was time for me to go. He sent me away with kisses as I went out into the sun. Again, I was taken to the spa. This time they placed me in a new room with shadows dancing on the ceiling. Again I lay down on a table, but on my back. A small girl came in with big eyes.

She turned on soft music and told me to close my eyes. It wasn't long until she had pulled all my hair tightly back so it wouldn't get ruined. Creams and oils and salts were rubbed along my face. She was gentle throughout. After a second wash, she placed on something heavier and left it there. Instead of just leaving me there, she massaged something onto my arms.

Ten minutes passed before she took out a machine to really scrub the stuff off my face. The girl patted it down after she was done to remove anything she missed, which wasn't enough to be noticed. She had me stand and go into a new room. There were several large, cushioned chairs in front of tubs. I was seated toward the back. She filled the tub with warm water and turned on the vibrations in the chair.

Another girl took her place to give me a pedicure. After a while of pampering, she finally painted them maroon and painted white skulls on the big toes. My eyes widened. She claimed it was requested. I chuckled, knowing who had. She put sandals on my feet and took me to another location. Again, I was seated, but this time, my nails were done.

They were French tips—with black paint, another request special from Lucifer. Thankfully there weren't any extra designs. I went to go, but again my location were changed. They gave me a sandwich and water. Instead of arguing, I ate. I finished quickly and they took me to get my hair done. They washed it completely so it shined brightly.

To top it off, they made it completely straight, adding a few inches. The woman took several strands of hair from the front left. She braided and twirled it before adding a clip to the bottom. She did the same to the right. Lifting both braids, she laced them together in the back. When she had finished, we swapped places.

This time a man did my makeup. He didn't add enough so that I looked funny. The colors were very soft and faint. He smiled at his work the whole time. I sat patiently during all of it, wondering why I was being made over.

The final scene change took me to a wardrobe. A dark red dress was put on me. It was tight and went to my knees. The sleeves almost met my elbows. It was lovely, until the earrings were added. They were red studs coming out of a black skull. Black heels went on, and that was it.

They took me outside where, no joke, a black carriage was sitting with midnight horses. My first question was how, but then Lucifer walked out of its door. He had his hair slicked back and completely dark suit on. His hand extended, and I took it. He kissed my cheek and pulled me inside. It was fully red. I heard the horse neigh and pull away. Its clip-clop was muffled in the cab. Lucifer sat across from me.

"I have a very special evening planned. So I got this made for you."

He took out a medium, flat, square box. It had velvet touches when he opened it. My eyes grew to the size of ornaments as they ran over the necklace. Of course it was black, but very beautiful. The back had long, dark strands with the occasional loop in between. It stretched out, his name running along the left side, followed by a sword in the center, dripping red. On the right was my name. Attaching it all was a spider-web pattern. My jaw hung open, and his curled to grin.

He lifted it and came near. His fingers traced along my neck as he clipped it on. As he pulled his hand away, I kissed him. Ignoring the fact that my dress could rip, I moved closer to him quickly. He held tight but the carriage stopped. I heard him laugh before he opened the door. We were by the beach. The sun was setting over the ocean.

My eyes wandered down to the shore to see the water rolling over the sand. There stood several people, all dressed up. A black carpet stretched from where the carriage was to the gathering. Torches were set up around a wired entrance.

Lucifer pulled me out to my family. Audrey stood to the left of the priest, and Arthur was on the right. The rest of my family was seated, facing the beach. It was when they heard my heels click on the cement that they stood. Annilia rushed over to hand me a bouquet of actual flowers. Lucifer leaned into me so he could speak. "I want this to be done right. You can say no and walk away. No one has a gun to anything." My heart fluttered, and I could scarcely breathe.

I walked down the aisle again, and this time I truly smiled. We stood in front of everyone. Father looked happy as he held my mother's hand. All my siblings were scattered. Augustus had his kids and their mom. He must have told Father.

The priest began, just like before. Everything was almost the same. Before we got to the answers, Lucifer began to speak. He had actually made vows. "Valencia, since I've met you, something in me has changed. You've caused that change. You made me fall in love. I will never let anything tear us apart. Nothing will ever hurt you. I love you completely and want us to be forever." I didn't get to speak. The priest began, and Lucifer said, "I do." It was my turn too fast. When I said the words, I meant them.

The kiss wasn't forced. It was deep and perfect. He released me first, so I could hug Audrey. In her ear I whispered about the wing change. Her arms got tighter. She knew me very well. I pulled away to hug everyone else. We walked down to where torches were scattered around a table.

Plates sat stacked high with lasagna. Everyone had a glass of wine. We all took a seat. This time, I didn't down the wine, only sipped at it. After a while, everyone shared what was going on in their lives. I finally got to meet my niece and nephew on a personal level.

"How is the happy couple?" Beatrice's words rang through my head. Something in me growled. She had been with my husband.

His hand dug into my thigh to keep me silent. "We have been extraordinary. She told me she loves me, last night." Everyone clapped, and Father winked. Audrey was baffled beyond words.

We all dug in. It was still hot, even though it must have been sitting there awhile. The melted cheese was delicious. The sauce was perfect. My plate was cleaned to the point that it could be used again and not taste like lasagna. I emptied my glass as I listened to the soft noises of everyone finishing.

It was time for good-byes. Lucifer let me stay long enough to hug and kiss everyone before he scooped me up and took me to the carriage. We went back to our room in a real marriage. Again, champagne was waiting for us, but this time rose petals were scattered everywhere. He had made this night spectacular.

Epilogue

I finished the week in Hawaii with my husband, exploring the island and each other. When we did get home, he had a room set up in the tower so I could do anything I wanted. Paints and a canvas sat on one side and books on the other. Audrey would visit. She left Mark's music box one day so I could listen to it.

It didn't take long for a routine to fall into place. Lucifer started working again. Some days, I would awake to breakfast, but, if I was lucky, he would wake me just to say good-bye. He would return around nightfall, unless he came back early. When he was gone, I could do anything I wanted inside the castle. Even though I was willing to stay, they feared me leaving. I almost always shared lunch with Audrey or Annilia. Mother would ask, but I hadn't said yes. Father would stop by, though, to check on me. Ezekiel would occasionally fly into my tower room to say hi. It was Augustus who had moved out to be with his children.

A month after the wedding, I had started getting sick and fat. My period hadn't arrived, only escalating my worries. I was declared pregnant. For angels, babies grow fast; Lucifer tried to stay and help when I wasn't well, but he just couldn't. Everyone congratulated me and promised a party. I only sat in the tower and cried. I didn't know who the father was. Audrey offered to perform an ancient tradition with the wedding ring to determine the gender, but she couldn't help with anything else.

In the corner of the bedroom, Lucifer had started handcrafting a crib. He was working on it slowly, knowing it'd be awhile but I could hear the construction taking place down the hall. A room was being set up but not painted. They would bring me to Earth in a month or two to see Mark and tell him. Also, they urged me to get an ultrasound. Then we would see not only if it was boy or girl, but also if it had wings. We would find out the color at birth. If it had no wings, I was dead.

About the Author

My name is Nicole Brollier, and I am a teenager. For years, I have moved around, seeing new places and meeting new people. Each school is an undiscovered place, loaded with secrets and experiences. In some way, all that I have gone through is laced into a story I pulled from my imagination. On my travels, I uncover new backdrops while friends bring to life parts of the characters I have been missing. In each encounter, I am able to weave my life into a tale to express who I am and how I truly feel. Each emotion is from my heart—each experience dictates an event my brain remembers, but it is my soul that enlightens the story, bringing every character and setting to life.

About the Book

Valencia has lived with her aunt since she was one. She is half-angel and half-demon, but her angelic soul is framed for treason. Of all bad things to possibly happen to someone so innocent, she is declared guilty. Before they can deliver punishment, she falls to Earth, where she finds true love trapped under a tree. But with no warning, her neglectful father returns, tearing her away to live a new life under the control of a powerful demon.